T0196324

Little Bits of Joy

& wisdom from a very good dog

Dena Plotner Mumm

authorHOUSE®

AuthorHouse™
1663 Liberty Drive
Bloomington, IN 47403
www.authorhouse.com
Phone: 1 (800) 839-8640

Published by AuthorHouse   05/08/2017

ISBN: 978-1-5246-9129-5 (sc)
ISBN: 978-1-5246-9128-8 (e)

Library of Congress Control Number: 2017907037

Print information available on the last page.

Contents

Em"bark"ing On A New Mission – Writing Brinkley's Story

It's been an idea of mine for a long time…long before we lost Brinkley in July of 2013, and since then, it has become a sort of mission for me…to record the story of this little dog we loved so much. "Loved", past tense, is, of course, not accurate at all, because we love him still. Every week when I dust the little round box covered with pictures of red roses, where Brinkley's ashes reside, I kiss the top of the box and say "I love you, Brinkley…I love you forever". It was an idea of mine even before I read the wonderful book "Bliss To You", co-written by renowned author Dean Koontz and his beloved golden retriever, Trixie, but I believe that reading this book helped to reinforce in my mind the need to write the story of my beloved cocker spaniel, both from his perspective and my own. I was so overcome after reading Trixie's book that I wrote to Mr. Koontz, and he was so incredibly gracious that he wrote back, sending me a signed and personalized copy of his latest novel, "Relentless", featuring "a Lassie who is not a collie, but don't underestimate her!" Indeed, I think it unwise to underestimate the many and varied abilities of any dog, most especially their innate ability to love unconditionally, to make us smile on our worst of days, and to lift us above the more base instincts of our humanity up to their level. God certainly had our best interests at heart when he paired us with the dog. And some dogs just seem to have a lot to say, and the ability to do so without fumbling with words as we do. Brinkley was such a dog. It is my dream that I might be able to share Brinkley's heart with others as Mr. Koontz did with Trixie, but even if not, in writing this book I will have recorded his story for myself and everyone who fell in love with him to keep forever. And that, in itself, will be reward enough; to honor this very good dog who gave us his all, and who taught us so much as well.

Dena Plotner Mumm, 2017

Dedication – For Taffy, Murphy & Moxie – Those Who Came Before & After

In addition to Brinkley, I have had three other wonderful cocker spaniels. I have loved each of them just as much, and all for their own unique personalities. This book is for them as well.

Taffy was my childhood companion and "little brother"...I begged for a dog for some time (it seemed like forever to me!) before my parents relented and got me one. It was late summer, 1972, and I was nine years old when Taffy came home to live with us, and it had to be the happiest thing that ever happened to me. And our relationship never got to be something I just took for granted after the initial thrill of bringing a puppy home. I was an only child, so Taffy became my best buddy and we spent many, many happy years together. Taffy liked tuna salad on toast, steak bones, and ice cream, but not if you sliced a banana on top...if you did that, he would pick off the banana slices and lay them on the floor! He helped us build our sun porch, carrying little triangles of wood around the yard as they fell from the sawhorses. He also liked to play board games, especially the "pop dice" version of "Sorry", which seemed

3

to fascinate him as he laid on the other side of the board, proving to be a worthy opponent! We grew up together, playing outside, enjoying the sunshine, listening to music… just generally inseparable. He had a wonderful, long life, and was just a month shy of seventeen when he left us to journey on to Rainbow Bridge in 1989, but I still miss him as though I just lost him. What a happy day it will be when I finally see him again!

Murphy was my second cocker spaniel, and Tim and I got him in 1989, after two years of marriage and following the loss of Taffy and Tim's cat, Charlie. The two of them passed within three months of one another, so what a joyful event it was, not only for Tim and me, but for my parents as well, when we brought little red Murphy home in October of that year! He was a beautiful puppy and had a lovable little feisty attitude to go with his good looks! He came home to the house on Coventry, where his Daddy built him a custom pen in the front of the garage, complete with a doghouse, carpeting (courtesy of Grandpa), and a place for potty papers at the other end! He even had heat and air conditioning to keep him comfortable, no matter what the season. When we moved to Brookshire, Murphy became Grandma's dog, and spent many happy days helping her with gardening chores in their big back yard. On one of our trips to Michigan, we found a bandana for Murphy which proclaimed "I'm Grandma's Dog", and he wore it proudly; and I think Grandma was pretty proud of him, too! Murphy had a stroke when he was eleven years old which left him with a little tilty head, but we found it adorable. At that time we made the decision to move our bedroom downstairs so we could be close to him at night, and I can still see him lying there next to the bed with his little head cocked, waiting for us to join him. When he had to be hospitalized for a few days in his last months, Tim went over at night to walk him around outside the emergency clinic, and he still had enough spunk to bark at the train that always rolled through town at that time. Now when we hear that train, we call it "Murphy's train", and I like to envision him riding through town on the caboose, his little tail wagging, barking happily!

After Brinkley's passing in July of 2013, we just felt lost. I didn't know if I was ready for another puppy and my Mom didn't think we were either, but Tim felt that it would be the best thing for all of us to see if we could find a new little buddy as soon as possible. And we did…on Taffy's birthday, on the internet! The breeder was in Miller, Missouri, and we made the trip in late July and brought little Moxie home with us. He has proven, like Murphy, to be a true redhead, and has half a blue eye on the left side which I think contributes to his orneriness! He is our liveliest boy to date, with springs for back legs, so he has kept things hopping (no pun intended!) around our house! As I near the completion of writing this book, Moxie is already approaching four years old and we have many favorite stories about him as well, but my personal favorite is the one that earned him the title of "Hero" in my eyes. Moxie and I were sitting on the front porch, where all our boys have loved to be, when one of the three outdoor neighbor cats came walking through our side yard, down the driveway, and across the street towards home. As he made the crossing, Moxie ran down the porch and growled at him, as he does whenever he sees any of the cats, and when the cat turned, we saw that he had a bird in his mouth. However, Moxie's growl caused the cat to hesitate, and as he did he released his grip on the bird, which flew out of his mouth and up into the branches of our front yard tree! I was so proud of Moxie for saving the life of that bird that I immediately hailed him as a hero and savior of birds! And that little bird appreciated Moxie's efforts on his behalf, too, because he stopped by the next day when we were sitting on the back deck to say thank you. I am convinced that it was the same little dove that Moxie saved, because I will never forget the beautiful sight of him spreading his wings and flying to safety. And I believe he knew that he had Moxie to thank for saving his life. So, all of my boys have had distinct and very special personalities, and every one of them has stolen our hearts, for so many reasons they are impossible to count.

And so, Taffy, Murphy, and Moxie, this book is for Brinkley and all of you as well. And Taffy and Murphy, I can't wait to see you again at our joyful reunion at Rainbow Bridge…that will be the happiest day of my life when I see my boys come running to greet me once more, knowing we will never be separated again.

Brinkley's Introduction
– First Impressions

My name is Brinkley Mumm, but that's not how I started out. Mommy and Daddy didn't find out until the day they picked me up to take me to my new home, but that day my breeder asked Mommy, "So, what are you going to name him?" Mommy responded that my name would be Brinkley, which, by the way, is a name that she and Daddy got from the movie "You've Got Mail", starring Meg Ryan and Tom Hanks. In that movie, Tom Hanks' character has a golden retriever named Brinkley, and since my brother, Murphy, also a cocker spaniel, had been named after the lead character in another favorite movie, "Murphy's Romance", and my step-brother Indy, a sun conure, had been named after the Indiana Jones movies, Mommy liked the idea of naming me after the dog they had loved in "You've Got Mail". Lois, my breeder, seemed impressed and said "That's a nice name…I've just been calling him Joe." But Mommy had already picked up on the fact that I was no ordinary dog. Not to mention there was already a Joe Cocker down the street, a black and white cocker, whereas I am golden brown. And not that Joe Cocker is not in itself a very clever name, a name which always causes people to smile; it's just that, as you will see, it doesn't quite suit my personality. And having already paid me a couple visits, Mommy could tell that.

I can't say that I have the clearest memory of the very first visit, when Daddy came to see me by himself, because my eyes were still closed. I was only ten days old when Daddy stopped by to see me for the first time. When Lois brought me outside and Daddy patted my tiny little head, I started squirming a bit and making little whimpering noises to let him know that I could already tell that I liked him and the idea of becoming a part of their family. Daddy took several pictures of me to take back to Mommy since she couldn't come with him that first time. I don't think I was at my most photogenic on that first visit but Daddy must have liked what he saw, because he told Lois he would like to adopt me. No big surprise they picked me, I guess, because I was preceded in their home by Murphy the cocker spaniel. Also, Mommy was an only human child, but she has told me that when she was nine years old, my grandparents tired of hearing her beg and plead for a dog and adopted a cocker spaniel themselves, my uncle Taffy. Daddy had also grown up with cocker spaniels, so it seemed natural to add me to that lineage.

I think we all have a clear recollection of Mommy and Daddy's first visit together, their fourteenth wedding anniversary and the day before I turned four weeks old. When Mommy came in, it was love at first sight. I can say that for sure, because my eyes were wide open by now, and big, brown and soulful. Lois put me on Mommy's lap and we spent the next hour visiting and bonding. Daddy took a lot of pictures of us to show my grandparents when we returned home that night, and they were in full agreement about bringing me into the family. As I understand it, when Murphy was seven years old, the house next door to Grandma and Grandpa went up for sale, so Mommy and Daddy bought it. So I have the ideal situation of living right next door to my grandparents and being a shared dog, something that has brought all of us incredible joy over the years. But, more about that later! When the hour had passed and Lois took me off of Mommy's lap to return me to my dog mom, Gina Louise, I cried just a little to let Mommy know that I would miss her until she returned. I had already bonded with my human mommy, but it wouldn't be time for me to go home with her until I was a little older.

Mommy and Daddy returned to visit me again when I was six weeks old, and this time when Mommy entered the house, I heard her sharp intake of breath and the exclamation that I had become a little bundle of curls over the last two weeks! It made me happy that she liked my new, curly coat, which made me smile for my pictures that day. Mommy and Daddy stayed with me an hour at that visit too, but this time when they left they promised that at their next visit, in two more weeks, I could come home with them! It was a long two weeks for all of us, but nice to know that soon I would be joining them in my new forever home!

Little Bits Of Joy – Always Play With Your Food

When I came home to live with Mommy and Daddy in my new forever home, I came with a sense of humor, already capable of some pretty funny ways of entertaining myself, and, as it turned out, my new family as well! One sure way I learned to make everybody laugh was to play with my kibble. You see, dogs, like children, know that it's fun to play with our food, and I liked to keep mealtimes fun by doing so. I would begin by inspecting the kibble in the bowl and then I would start to dance around it, raring up on my little back legs and acting as if I were going to pounce on it. My Grandma made the observation that I looked like a little Lipizzaner stallion, and everyone seemed to thoroughly enjoy the act, which encouraged me to keep playing with my food into adulthood. At that point, I also discovered a way to get everyone else in on the game. Now when I want to engage one of my human family members in play at mealtime, I just start acting silly about the chow in the bowl, as if to say, "Oh, no…I don't want THAT!" and accompany it with a toss of my head, or a turn as if to run off and chase the kibble one piece at a time. And they fall for it every time, throwing pieces of food one at a time for me to chase and eat! Sometimes they try to complain about it, especially when they are on their busy work schedules and don't have time to play and be silly, but I think it is more important for them to learn to relax and enjoy the game; to get out of the rat race, even just for a few moments. If there is one thing every good dog knows, it's the importance of getting our humans to have a bit of fun, and playing with my food proves to be a sure way to do that, even on our busiest of days!

What Brinkley Taught Me About...Starting Over

Talk about God's timing...Brinkley was born on the day that Murphy stopped eating. Murphy was our twelve year old light red cocker spaniel, and had been the joy of our existence all of those years. When he was eleven years old, he had a stroke which left him with a little tilted head, and we found it adorable, especially so when he would go into our new downstairs bedroom and lay next to the bed waiting for us to join him, his sweet little head cocked to one side and those big, brown cocker spaniel eyes. Later that year he got very sick, and landed in the emergency hospital over Memorial Day weekend, diagnosed with pancreatitis. He had become reluctant to eat, and we finally resorted to cooking for him....soft foods, easy to digest, like chicken and dumplings or mashed potatoes. We managed to keep him with us into August, and he turned twelve years old on August 2nd. Then on August 20th, he stopped eating altogether. He couldn't be coaxed into eating anything, even foods that he had previously loved. We could tell he was in a lot of pain by then, and we were faced with the toughest decision we had ever had to make...to release him from his pain and allow him to make the journey to Rainbow Bridge, where all good pets go to await their human families in Heaven. We already had a cocker spaniel there, my childhood brother, Taffy, who had come to live with us when I was nine years old and had attained the incredible age of one month shy of seventeen years. We also had a cat there, Charlie, who belonged to my husband, Tim, when we got married. After our marriage, Taffy remained with my Mom and Dad since that was where he had spent his entire life, and Charlie lived with Tim and me. 1989 was a tough year, with Taffy's passing in June and Charlie's in September. But then we adopted Murphy in October of that year and he completed our little family of three until his step-brother, our sun conure, Indy, joined our family in January of 1991.

In the weeks leading up to Murphy's passing, a praying mantis came to live in a potted flower on our back deck. My Grandma had enjoyed talking with me about the praying mantis when I was a child, because she was a deeply religious woman and pointed out to me how the insect indeed seemed to be praying. We knew that Murphy was sick, and felt as if the praying mantis was keeping a vigil with us. He lingered for several weeks, then a few days after Murphy's passing, he disappeared and we never saw him again, but I will always be grateful for how he kept us company over the course of those last few weeks, and thankful to God for sending him.

Murphy left us on a Thursday night, August 23rd, 2001. We called in to our workplaces that Friday, unable to go in due to the depth of our grief. That weekend we felt lost without the little shadow who had followed us everywhere, and on Sunday Tim decided to call the breeder where we had gotten Murphy. She no longer had any pups left from her most recent litter, but referred us to another breeder whom she shared dogs with, stating that Lois and Lyle had just had a litter of puppies. When Tim contacted Lois, she told us that her litter had been born on August 20th, just four days prior to Murphy's passing, and the very day that Murphy had stopped eating. I felt that Murphy must have known that little Brinkley had been born and that it was now okay for him to leave us; and that soon Brinkley would be able to step in and assume care of his human family. Dogs possess a sense of intuition that we cannot fathom, and I believe that he knew the point in time when he could depart, and that we would be all right.

When Brinkley was ten days old, Tim had to make a trip to the Bloomington area, where Brinkley's breeder lived. He called to see if he could stop by and see the puppies, and Lois agreed. She brought little Brinkley outside in the palm of her hand, and Tim got his first look at his new little son, eyes still closed up tight. He patted his little head and took some pictures of him to bring home to show me, since I was unable to make that first visit with him. As with all ten day old puppies, he didn't have many recognizable features of a cocker spaniel yet, but we fell in love with him and asked if we could adopt him into our family. We also made arrangements to visit him at four weeks and six weeks so we could all get acquainted. I still feel that was an important step in easing his transition from the breeder's home to ours, and one of the main reasons that we had such an incredibly strong bond with him.

As luck would have it, Brinkley was to be four weeks old one day after our fourteenth wedding anniversary. I could think of nothing I would rather do to celebrate than to run over to Bloomington, visit my new baby, and then stop for dinner at Bennigan's, a favorite restaurant of ours. When we arrived, we sat at Lois and Lyle's kitchen table and Lois brought little Brinkley to me and put him on my lap. By this time he really looked like a cocker spaniel, and was so adorable! He was alert, looking up at me as if to say, "Are you my Mommy?" Tim took lots of pictures of us so we could show my Mom and Dad their new little grandson. We visited for an hour and got to see Brinkley's sister; she was as feminine as Brinkley was all boy. We have a picture of Lois holding both puppies. Brinkley's sister was black with a little spot of white on her chin, and about half the size of Brinkley. Brinkley has his little back legs crossed, a habit that he maintained throughout his life. He liked to lay on his stomach with his back feet crossed behind him, which I found absolutely precious, to the degree that I took close-up photos of his little paddy paws for his scrapbook. When Lois took Brinkley off my lap to return him to his dog mom, he gave me a little whimper, as if to let me know that he had already bonded with me, and I knew for sure that I was already in love with him! Tim and I left with the agreement to come back for a second visit in a couple weeks, and had a nice anniversary dinner at Bennigan's, made even better due to the excitement about our new little guy. And the excitement continued when we returned home…Tim printed out the photos he had taken with his phone to show my Mom and Dad, and they were thrilled with him too!

In two weeks, we returned to Lois and Lyle's to pay Brinkley another visit, and he continued to surprise us with the way he was growing and changing each time. At this visit, I practically squealed with delight when I saw him…

in just two weeks his coat had turned into a mass of golden curls! I think he knew how pleased I was with this new development, because in some of the pictures from this visit, he looks like he is smiling! We stayed with him an hour at this visit too, and when we left this time we knew that we would be able to bring him home with us when we returned the next time. I couldn't wait until that next two weeks passed!

On October 20th, 2001, we left home early to go and pick up our golden boy. Upon arrival, I noticed yet another change, but this time I wasn't delighted…Brinkley seemed to be very itchy, and was busy scratching as we were getting ready to bring him home. I figured he had picked up some fleas, so I wasn't too alarmed, but also not too happy, having dealt with fleas when we had Murphy. At that time we lived on Coventry Drive, and the back of our house connected with a large open field, so we had fleas in abundance. We had to resort to flea dips and bombing the house on several occasions, and the fleas also took a liking to me, which was most unpleasant. But nothing could spoil the joy of bringing our baby home, and when we got there we called my Mom and Dad to come and meet him, and they came over straightaway. Brinkley nibbled on everyone with his little puppy teeth, and we have pictures of him tasting everyone's fingers on that first day at home. My Aunt Jean also came over to see him that first day, and we spent some time on his new front porch. When we moved in to the house next door to my parents on Brookshire East, the porch was open, with three large, white colonial style pillars. Tim decided that we should enclose the porch with a railing so Murphy could enjoy being out front without a leash, so he measured Murphy's shoulders to ensure that he couldn't get through the railing and built a wonderful porch rail with round white spindles. Murphy had loved laying out there with his head on the bottom railing, watching any activity that might be happening, and we were sure that Brinkley would love it too. However, Brinkley was so small when he came home that Tim had to put up a small fence around the perimeter to make sure he couldn't get out between the spindles! When Aunt Jean came over I was sitting out front reading a book with baby Brinkley on my lap...he had had a big day and was starting to get sleepy. Before he left Lois and Lyle's, they had him trimmed up a bit, and he had an adorable rounded tuft of hair on top of his head which resembled a little crown. And that was fitting, because he had already become the prince of my heart!

We started Brinkley out at a different vet than where we had taken Murphy. Murphy had done well with his vet until an unfortunate event which happened when we moved in on Brookshire. I had known the original owner of our home since I was a child because I had grown up next door, and after we moved in and got settled, she wanted to come by and see the house. When she stopped by with her son in law we put Murphy in the back yard since he could be temperamental with strangers. We weren't expecting the former owner to suddenly go out the back patio door to see the swimming pool since we had remodeled it, but before we could stop her, she was out there, abruptly putting her hand down to pet Murphy, and in fear, he bit her hand. That was an awful experience, especially since we had plans to go out and eat that night since it was our eighth wedding anniversary. Instead, Jan headed off to the emergency room for treatment of a dog bite, and was required to file a report against our precious Murphy. Instead of dinner out that night, I remember sitting on the stairway of our new home in tears, worried that we might be asked to have our dog put down for biting someone when it really wasn't his fault. Luckily that didn't happen, but it did make our vet wary of Murphy. At his next exam, the vet made reference to his bite record by saying, "Well, we know we really can't trust you now." I was deeply insulted by this, especially coming from a vet, who you would think would understand such a situation from the dog's perspective. That scenario was exacerbated when Murphy became very ill the Friday before Memorial Day, and when Tim arrived at our vet's office with him, he was turned away because they were closing for the long holiday weekend. At that time, we began taking him to the Animal Emergency Clinic here in town, and met up with a wonderful lady named Tracei who was not in the least bit afraid of Murphy. The first time she met him, she got down on the floor with him, got right in his face and loved on him, and he responded in kind, because a dog can always recognize a kindred spirit.

But, back to Brinkley's itching. Our new vet examined him when he first came home and all seemed well. She didn't detect any fleas. However, about a month after we brought Brinkley home, his itching had only worsened, finally to the point that he couldn't rest, and therefore there was no rest for me either. And I had begun itching myself. My right foot itched so intensely that I had rubbed it vigorously on the carpet trying to get relief, and it had turned red and swollen up so that I could not wear even my loosest shoe. The day before Thanksgiving I had to call in sick to work to take Brinkley to the vet and myself to the doctor. Turns out that Brinkley had come home with sarcoptic mites, which are invisible to the naked eye and visible only under a microscope. Lucky for us, we now had a great new vet, and she got him diagnosed and feeling better fast. And a round of antibiotics got me back on my feet again as well. I will never forget that Wednesday night, the night before Thanksgiving…Tim and I usually went out to eat that evening with his family so we could spend Thanksgiving Day with my folks, but I was unable to go that year. I was sitting in our kitchen, eating a Stouffer's frozen dinner and watching little Brinkley entertain himself by pulling on a strand of a dish scrubby, which he had somehow pulled out underneath the kitchen cabinet door. He kept on task with that the whole time I was eating my dinner off a TV tray, and I was so happy that he had found something to keep him busy for a while, because I was worn out from being up with the little guy and his itchies during the night!

We had gotten through the first month of having a new puppy in the house, and I was reminded of what a difference a puppy presents after dealing with a senior dog! But it was all joy…pure joy!

Little Bits Of Joy – Dances With Fireflies

Kevin Costner may have enjoyed dances with wolves, but since there were no wolves (thankfully!) near my new home, I invented my own version, "Dances with Fireflies". My first summer with my new family, I noticed that Mommy was enamored with these little insects that blink light as they fly. She would go outside as dusk was turning to dark on evenings in mid to late June just to observe them, and she would look down into that deep brown gaze of mine and say, "Brinkley, only God could come up with something as delightful as a firefly!" And while she never tried to catch one, she would just sit quietly and enjoy the twinkling of their lights all over the back yard, I was still a puppy and a bit more exuberant. Eager to express my shared appreciation of the lightning bugs, I began to dance with them; not in an aggressive manner, but as light on my feet as a ballet dancer, I would jump into the air, performing a little twirl as I sought to reach them, and on occasion, I would catch one in my mouth! Mommy was quick to say, "Oh, no, Brinkley, don't eat them!" and I confess, I really never intended to, but lightning bugs are slow flyers, and sometimes I was just a bit too fast for them. And in spite of Mommy's dismay when I would catch one, I could detect the joy bubbling just under the surface of her demeanor in response to my dancing. And as every good dog knows, bringing joy to our human companions is a mission we take very seriously. That is, until we catch them smiling and letting go of their cares, and then we can do the same!

What Brinkley Taught Me About... Appreciating The Little Things

If you ask my husband, Tim, he will tell you that at some point in time, we forgot how to relax. And I would have to agree. Our lives have always revolved around our careers, and when we are not at our jobs, we obsess about things around our house. Every weekend finds me cleaning house, keeping up with what seems to be a constant list of chores and errands to ensure that our home remains organized and tidy, that we have food in the cupboards and refrigerator, that our pets are fed and cared for, laundry is done, and well, every woman can relate to trying to stay ahead of all these tasks! And Tim keeps busy with all of the outdoor work needed to maintain the yard, mowing the grass, watering the many pots of flowers he takes such pride in planting every year, keeping up with the pool (our 20,000 gallon science experiment, as he likes to call it), and also handling the myriad of other issues that crop up around the house, such as cleaning out the gutters, raking leaves in the fall, and plowing snow in the winter. It's enough to make you lose your cool on occasion, and it can literally take up every day off, leaving little or no time to kick back and relax. Unless you have a wise little dog to help you remember just how important it is to make time to do so!

Since Tim built the railing around the front porch when we first moved in and had little Murphy, Brinkley was the lucky recipient of a big, fenced porch to run around on, and he was out there with us immediately after coming home… that is, after we made some necessary modifications to the railing so he couldn't escape between the spindles while he was growing up. He loved being out there and watching everything and everyone, and it became one of his favorite places to hang out, just like it always has been for us. And just like we have found it to be, Brinkley found it to be a perfect place to relax, kick back, and enjoy a nice day, or even a rainy day, since the porch is completely covered and we can sit out there no matter what the weather. Sometimes Brinkley would lie on the concrete, which I'm sure was nice and cool against his tummy, and often when he did that, he would rest his chin on the bottom board of the porch railing so he could keep an eye on things through the spindles. Brinkley also liked sitting on the porch furniture, and he would jump up on the rocking chairs, double rocker, or even the stationary wicker chairs in order to get a better vantage point on whatever might be happening in the neighborhood. It was when we got Brinkley that I began the tradition of having my birthday photo taken each year sitting with the little guy on the double rocker. I have always found it easier to relax and smile when sitting next to my dog, so this became the ideal way to chronicle each year as it passed, with my best buddy sitting beside me and my arm around his furry shoulders. I have many photos of Brinkley on his front porch, everything from a picture of him sitting in the wicker chair sporting what looks like, for all practical purposes, a big, happy smile, to a beautiful photo taken at sunset of him laying on one of the rockers with his sweet, contented face on the wooden arm of the chair, gazing off into the distance, the very image of peaceful repose. And because Brinkley was so happy on our porch, it increased our enjoyment of that space all the more, and we spent many, many wonderful hours out there soaking up the fresh air and sunshine, savoring nature, and just watching the world go by. And since Tim and I have always had such a difficult time disciplining ourselves to just be still, it is really saying something that Brinkley could help us achieve that state of relaxation and to sustain it for such an extended period of time without continually thinking of things to jump up and do. There is just something so calming about the quiet presence of a dog nearby...something so very beneficial to our restless spirits that only a dog can provide.

When we weren't hanging out together on the porch, Brinkley was my companion and photography assistant on the nature walks that became such an area of interest for me when I was creating my Bright Spots greeting card line. One spring in particular started that whole venture, because it got warm very early that year, around the first of March, and all the crocuses, tulips, hyacinths and daffodils began to bloom. And best of all, unlike so many springs where we have a brief warm spell and then it gets cold again and kills everything off, this year it stayed warm, so we just progressed from one beautiful crop of flowers to the next, and since everything was so lush and green and gorgeous, Brinkley and I made it our mission to share our nature photos with everyone we sent cards to that year. And then, since the handmade cards seemed to be such a hit with everyone we sent them to, I had to continue to look for new material to photograph, and that became quite an undertaking for the two of us! Our neighbor, Becky, who fell in love with Brinkley since her house was on our walk route, was also quite a gardener, so we made frequent stops at her house to photograph unusual flowers there, and she would even call us if she had a particularly beautiful specimen that she wanted to tell us about. We took many stunning photos there, including endless varieties of daylilies, irises, and alliums. We also enlarged our territory to search out new places to photograph, and over the course of time I developed a scrapbook of all my best photos that people could browse through if they were interested in ordering cards or artwork with a specific theme. And we utilized elements in our own yard, as well as Mom and Dad's yard, since they are also gardeners extraordinaire. My most beautiful hydrangea photos were all taken right next door, as they have every color of hydrangea in the rainbow, and hydrangeas are also like the mood ring of flowers, changing color as the blossoms age. Mom and Dad also have a great variety of daylilies, and some of the most stunning garden statuary imaginable, from the cute and winsome to the elegant and inspirational. I photographed their adorable little ladybugs and frogs, sweet cherubs and beautiful fairies and angels, which added yet another dimension to my greeting cards and artwork. I also took photos around our yard, including three smooth stones engraved with the words Faith, Hope and Love. These rocks were great individually and as a group, and I used those photos for both cards and artwork, including a framed piece incorporating the words of 1 Corinthians 13, "And now these three remain, faith, hope and love, but the greatest of these is love," with the three photos of the rocks in place of the words Faith, Hope and Love and the rest of the wording lettered in calligraphy. Brinkley and I were just about out of ideas and territory we could cover on our nature hikes when my Mom began making fairy gardens, and that opened up a whole new world in terms of our photography interests! My Mom has always been extremely talented in all the arts and crafts, and we were constantly into some creative pursuit when I was growing up, so when the fairy garden trend began, Mom was on the cutting edge, and I'm not just being prejudiced when I say that her gardens made the examples in the stores look downright lame! The very first one she made was a birthday gift for me, and we used it as a table centerpiece for our family Easter dinner that year, and from that point on, she was unstoppable! She made gardens for her home and for ours, as well as for my aunt and some of her most special friends. And I photographed them all, from shots showing the entire garden to little vignettes of each separate fairy and the nearby elements. I feel that these close-ups made the very best cards, and because she made so many gardens, I always had lots of new material to work with, which was wonderful! And it was great to have access to all of it so close to home so I didn't have to walk Brinkley's little legs off!

In addition to the front porch and our nature walks, Brinkley also enjoyed being outside on his back deck and in his back yard. He loved it out there right from the start, and Tim made sure that everything was safe for him as soon as we brought him home. Just like the railing on the front porch, we had to put some special, small fencing around the bottom of the pool fencing to ensure that the little guy couldn't slip through and get into the pool area when he was a puppy, and we have some really cute pictures of Brinkley in his little blue puppy harness trying to help his Dad put up the new fencing! Since we couldn't bring Brinkley home until October 20th, he didn't have a very long time to enjoy his new yard that first year, but that first fall we did put a crate cushion out on the deck for him to lay on, and he liked spending time out there chewing on strips of rawhide. And as I recall, Brinkley entered the "catch me, catch me" phase of his puppyhood in the winter, at about six months of age, and he also adored snow…I think this is universal among dogs! So, he would be out there playing in the snow, and I would be trying to coax him back inside so I could get on my way to work, and he would get up right near the back door and then take off again, with me yelling for him to get inside NOW! And of course, he would stay just out of reach and range, which was of course maddening and yet pretty cute at the same time, especially to see him standing there with snow on his nose, just teasing me as if to ask why I couldn't just lighten up and play with him, because, after all, isn't play far more important than going off to work? And I must admit, I wish that we all lived in a world where this truth is appreciated and observed, because the work would still be there at whatever time we arrived, right? There truly are many, many things that we humans would do well to learn from the superior wisdom of our dogs, if only we could admit it.

When Brinkley's first spring at home rolled around, we wasted no time getting back out in the yard, and Brinkley enjoyed the warm weather as much as we always do after a long Illinois winter spent cooped up in the house. And when that first June came we had an especially good crop of lightning bugs, which was great for a puppy's first spring, because like children, everything is new to them. And these little flashing bugs proved to be just delightful to Brinkley, as they always had been for me. Our observant little guy picked right up on the fact that these little creatures came out in force in his back yard just about sunset, and that they were rather low, slow fliers, and he found this very interesting indeed. And being that Brinkley was a pretty mellow little guy himself, he wasn't really interested in chasing them to catch them, but instead he would do a little leap-and-twirl kind of move that looked for all the world like he was dancing with the fireflies! Talk about cute...it was like a little ballet going on right there in our yard! I am pretty sure that someone was once quoted as stating that only God could come up with something as delightful as a firefly, and I would add to that statement that only God could create a little dog who would discover that it was wonderful fun to dance with them! And if I live to be one hundred, I will never forget the joy I felt in watching him do so!

Brinkley continued to love spending time in his back yard for his entire life, and we enjoyed the variety of every season out there with him. In spring and summer he would help Tim take care of the plants and pool (from the safe side of the fence, of course), in the fall we would rake up piles of leaves for him to run into (this was especially fun when he was small and would get lost in the middle of the pile!), and when we got deep snows in the winter Tim would run the snow blower out there to make paths for him. One year we got an exceptional blizzard and a couple feet of snow, and Brinkley had his own little maze of pathways that Tim made for him...and was he a happy dog out there running through them! The snow was so deep from that particular blizzard that the tops of the drifts were about at eye level for Brinkley, so not only were the paths that Tim created for him fun, they were a necessity for him to get out into his yard at all! And in every season, indeed practically every day, Brinkley would keep a trained eye on the gate leading through the pool area to the house next door where his Grandma and Grandpa live! He wanted to make sure that he never missed an opportunity to greet them whenever they stepped out the door, so he was ever-vigilant in watching that gate. It was a familiar sight for Tim and I to see his cute little cocker spaniel butt, complete with little nubby tail, facing in that direction! Brinkley was truly blessed to live his entire life next door to the other two people he loved most in all the world, and who loved him like the human grandchild they never had.

In addition to an enhanced appreciation of nature and all the simple things surrounding us that fill our lives with joy if only we take notice of them, Brinkley also taught us to appreciate time spent in the pursuit of absolutely nothing. I think that in the progressively busier-every-day world that we live in, this is a skill that perhaps can only be learned from a companion animal. Since it seems to be in the DNA of every human to have an agenda, whether it be to forge ahead in the workplace or just to keep up with things around the house, we are prone to be driven every moment to get something else done or to cross something else off our to-do list. Dogs are blessed in the fact that they don't have this obsession, and therefore they are great instructors of how to appreciate the priceless, and all-too limited, gift of time. Our pets are not consumed with worry about tomorrow, wondering how to please the boss in order to climb the corporate ladder, or even concerned with how to best accommodate the needs of their spouses, children or parents. Instead, they live blissfully in the moment, happy just to be near us, without a care about what we are doing, or not doing, with a sense of simple contentment that could benefit us more than a library full of self-help books. One has only to look into their eyes at such a moment to get a glimpse of that true peace that is so elusive to those of us born human. And because of the bond of love they have with us, how they must long to transmit that peace to us. Much like what we are instructed by the Scriptures to believe, their gaze seems to say to us, "Don't worry, Mom (or Dad), that concern of yours is only light and momentary and doesn't have any real and lasting significance in the big scheme of things, so come away with me, live in the moment, and I will help you see that what is truly important, what truly lasts forever, is what we have right here and now." What a gift they could bestow upon us if only it were not so fleeting… if only we could truly grasp and hold fast to it. But in just the same way that this concept is hard to get a handle on, time itself has a tendency to slip right through our fingers, so it would behoove most of us to put more effort into learning to really appreciate every moment given to us, hopefully before it is too late and we end up with regrets about all the years we have essentially lost in meaningless pursuits or patterns of non-constructive thought. I am preaching to the choir here because of all the people I know, I am one of the most guilty of worrying over things that may never happen, and of projecting my thoughts forward days or further ahead instead of just being happy in the moment. I'm not sure exactly what causes this type of behavior in certain individuals, but I'm guessing it has a lot to do with being somewhat of a control freak and wanting to have some sort of influence over the outcome of future events. What surprises me is that even though I now know that I have very little or even no control over how many things ultimately turn out, I am disappointed in how I still cling to those worrisome thought patterns. I guess it is true that old habits die hard, and maybe even for some of those habits, not at all, or at least not completely. And so I think that it has always been God's great and perfect plan for me to have a wise little dog to remind me that right now is what matters most. All of my dogs have helped me to live a bit more in the moment, and perhaps Brinkley most of all, due to his mellow, consistent temperament and his ability to accept the less desirable circumstances in life along with the better outcomes we strive for. Brinkley was always able to roll with the punches and take life one day at a time, even when life didn't always offer him the best of everything, which he so richly deserved for being such an angel, sent from God to teach us. So in this respect, I believe that even if we can't get a firm and lasting grip on how to truly appreciate each moment we are given in this life, God has made sure that we would have our pets to help us along the way...to help us, at least momentarily, to find those precious respites of peace when we find ourselves in turmoil...in those moments when our weary spirits need them most.

Little Bits Of Joy – A Dog Of Many Nicknames...& Costumes...& Expressions!

Mommy tells me that all of her boys have had lots of nicknames, and at least for my part, I can vouch for that! Most of mine have been sweet...things like Cuddle (or Snuggle) Bunny, Darlin', Baby Brinkley, Handsome Man, and so forth. I have on occasion earned myself an ornery nickname, such as when I have rolled in possum poop, which inspired Mommy to call me "Little Stinky Brinkey"! Brinkey (without the L), by the way, is Grandpa's nickname for me, and that is what Great Aunt Jean likes to call me as well. I have also been everything from Fuzzy Face (a nickname the Peanuts characters used for Snoopy in some of the old strips Mommy loved from when she was little) to Fuzzy Butt (a name which Daddy picked up from the Fuzzy Butz Pet Bakery in St. Joseph, Michigan). I even have a T-shirt from there that asks the rather personal question "Do you have a fuzzy butt?" Speaking of apparel, I have a vast array of that as well...not just T-shirts, but costumes galore! I have all kinds of getups, including a baseball cap, surf shorts (or "jams") complete with an opening to accommodate my tail, a soda jerk hat, a Sherlock Holmes cap, Easter Bunny ears, and reindeer antlers. I even have a pirate outfit that I wore for Halloween when Pirates of the Caribbean was the big film; Mommy's cousin Shari made the observation that I appeared to be a very sensitive pirate. I was just trying to channel Johnny Depp's soulful eyes and think I succeeded pretty well! And I have an Uncle Sam hat that Mommy puts on me for the Fourth of July, and I tolerate that far better than those noisy fireworks that all of our neighbors seem to enjoy. They say that dogs have expressive faces because we have eyebrows, but I have even more going for me than that. Mommy likes to laugh about the year she was Little Bo Peep for Halloween and I hurried to get in the picture with her and her sheep when Grandpa came over to take photos. Well, at first, Grandpa said "Get out of there, Brinkey, I'm taking a picture of your Mom!" So in that first photo, I look sad and bewildered because, after all, Grandpa NEVER talks to me like that. Then in the second photo, since he could tell that he had hurt my feelings, he said "Okay, Brinkey, you can stay", and in that picture I am smiling! And because I am such a good dog, I take a lot of pleasure in making everyone else smile too!

What Brinkley Taught Me About...
Having A Sense Of Humor

Since I have always believed it to be God's plan that I should have a dog, it seems especially so to lighten my moods and teach me how to laugh, whether at myself or just in general. My dogs have always been good teachers when the subject was humor, and Brinkley was certainly no exception! And he didn't have to work hard at being comical...sometimes it was just in his expressions! I have photos of Brinkley when he was just a puppy, and in some of them he has the cutest little crooked mouth which gave him a wide variety of different looks from photo to photo! In his first pictures by the Christmas tree in the living room, at the age of four months, he is laying on the tree skirt in front of one of my angel ornaments with that cute little expression, and in a subsequent shot he looks like he has the edge of one of the tree branches in his mouth, while all the while looking so absolutely innocent! And in another one of his puppy pictures, laying on the couch in the family room, he looks just like (and no, I'm not kidding...no one could make something like this up!)...old 60's-70's comedian Buddy Hackett!

Brinkley was also good at finding funny things to do, and even when you knew you shouldn't laugh, just like you shouldn't laugh when your two-year old says an inappropriate word, you couldn't help it! One event that stands out in my mind was when Brinkley decided that Tim's hosta bed in the back yard would be a good place to flop down for a rest! Being a plant man, Tim has always taken pride in landscaping the yard, so when I started laughing at Brinkley when I found him lying in the hostas, Tim was a little less amused than I! But it didn't take long for him, either, to get over his initial irritation and laugh about it too. You just couldn't deny the humor of the situation and how adorable he looked laying there in the flower bed! And the hostas were no worse for the wear since Brinkley took such a brief rest there; just long enough to cool down and then he was back up and on his way to his next adventure!

Another funny event occurred when Brinkley was just over a year old. That fall we repainted our kitchen cabinets, so Brinkley was out in the back yard to keep him from getting into the paint. At some point one of us looked up and noticed that Brinkley had jumped up on the bench outside our kitchen window like a little window-peeper so he could keep an eye on our progress! I guess since we always referred to him as the job foreman, he was just making sure he had a watchful eye on things. After all, Brinkley was very conscientious about his jobs around the house and always took his responsibilities about them seriously!

As previously stated, Brinkley never had to work hard at making us laugh, and perhaps the best testament to this fact is that Brinkley could even be funny when he was sleeping! Sometimes it was the positions he chose to nap in. One of his favorites was flat on his back with his legs in the air...Dad always said that meant it was going to rain, but I'm glad that wasn't always true, because if it had been we would have had rain just about every day! Tim always felt that laying on his back indicated that Brinkley was a very trusting dog. And I guess that might well have been the case because he certainly never had anything to fear in our home. Brinkley was the center of the universe and our lives revolved around him, which I feel is only right in a home where the family dog is loved as they deserve to be. Sometimes he would lay in positions that resembled Tim when he was sleeping, and I was able to capture pictures on some of these occasions! But perhaps the funniest thing that Brinkley came up with in terms of napping was WHERE he liked to nap...he had a particular fondness for our family room coffee table! We have a big, burled oak coffee table, very sturdy and low to the ground, and at a fairly early age, Brinkley decided that he liked to hop up there and lie on his side on the nice cool surface of that table! Well, it was another one of those situations where we probably should have corrected him and insisted that he jump down and find another spot, but it was just too funny! And for the most part, he never hurt anything that I might have had on the table as a centerpiece...he would just find a spot next to whatever it might be, and only once in a while would he bump into it at all. I do remember once when he jumped up onto the table with a little too much gusto and knocked off my white woodland Santa, breaking the nose of the fox in Santa's backpack! That never did get repaired so it looked very nice, but we knew it wasn't Brinkley's intention to hurt it. And that coffee table remained one of Brinkley's favorite places to nap for most of his life, until he had the leg surgery and could no longer make the leap. And I will never begrudge him for using our coffee table for his naps, because it was just one of many things that made Brinkley unique amongst all of my dogs, and that made life with him so endearing.

Brinkley was so easy-going and even-tempered that perhaps we took advantage of him. He hadn't been part of our family very long when we discovered that he was tolerant of costumes, so he had many of these over the course of his lifetime. He even participated with me, at home at least, in some of my Halloween costumes when I worked at Hobbico. Hobbico allowed us to dress up for Halloween and even held a contest each year for first, second and third place, and those of us in the advertising department usually scored well in these competitions. The first, and perhaps best, was the year we dressed up as Sesame Street characters, and I was Big Bird! There was something innately comical about me, the smallest member of the group, dressing up as the tallest character, but I think at least I did a pretty good job of making myself yellow from head to toe! I bought a yellow afro clown wig and cut feathers out of neon yellow poster board to stick out of the top, painted my face bright yellow and fashioned a beak out of the poster board, which I put over my nose with elastic cord. Then I got a quadruple extra-large sweatshirt, which went to my knees, a pair of brightly-colored striped socks, and borrowed a pair of yellow bird feet slippers from my hair dresser to complete the outfit! When I came outside to have pictures taken by my Mom before leaving for work on Halloween morning, Brinkley and Indy, our sun conure, looked at me as though they weren't even sure who I was! It was really quite hilarious! That year, our group, including other Sesame Street characters Bert and Ernie, Oscar the Grouch, Cookie Monster, Zoey, Elmo, and The Count, took first place in the competition, and I would say it was well-deserved, and a lot of fun besides!

Another year at Hobbico, a smaller group of us were fairy tale characters, including Wee Willie Winky, Peter, Peter, Pumpkin Eater, Little Red Riding Hood, and Little Bo Peep. I chose Little Bo Peep, and my Mom made me a pair of ruffled pantaloons and a ruffled apron and cap to wear with a denim dress I had. Suffice it to say I was a mass of ruffles that year, and the cap did nothing to enhance my round face! It made me very glad that it wasn't part of my daily attire! That year, Dad came over to get pictures of me holding my stuffed sheep, and little Brinkley ran over and sat down in front of me to be part of the photo! Well, Dad said, "Brinkey (this was always my Dad's name for Brinkley, to leave the "L" out, and we all used it that way at times as a term of endearment), get out of there, I'm taking a picture of your Mom!" So, in the first photo, the poor little guy looked puzzled, and even a bit downcast, over Grandpa's remark! So then Grandpa felt bad and said, "Okay, Brinkey, you can stay in the picture", so in the next photo Brinkley looked as though all was well with the world now that he had been given permission to stay in the shot with me! We all still laugh when we see those photos and remember sweet, sensitive little Brinkley, who loved having his picture taken when he was younger, so much so that he would run to be in the photo if someone got the camera out!

Since I have been a huge fan of the Lord of the Rings trilogy since reading the books in my early teens, I went crazy over the movies when director Peter Jackson filmed the trilogy. It was my idea to dress up as characters from the movies when they came out, so several of us dressed up as Gandalf the Grey, Frodo and Samwise, and Arwen Evenstar. I chose to be Frodo, and bought a pair of big, hairy feet to complete my look that year. As you might imagine, Brinkley found these feet fascinating! We had pictures taken sitting on the double rocker on our front porch that year, and in one of them, I have my legs crossed and little Brinkley is inspecting my furry Hobbit foot as if he thinks I have begun a transformation into becoming a real dog just like him! There is also a picture of him sitting next to me on the double rocker, and in this photo I am holding my Hobbit sword in one hand while having my other arm around Brinkley's shoulders. Mom thinks that photo looks like I am getting ready to take him out, and even though that was certainly not my intention, it is still a very funny picture to look back on!

Although not my personal best effort ever as a costume, one year the Hobbico group decided to be characters from Shrek, the popular movie about a pretty disgusting but lovable ogre and his family and friends. In this cast of characters, I chose to be the Donkey, which I didn't really have the personality to match, as he was rather loud and boisterous and I am neither! I wore a gray sweat suit with the hood up, a headband with donkey ears, a donkey snout, and even black gloves to make my hands look more like hooves. That year it was about 80 degrees on Halloween, so you can imagine how uncomfortable that costume was by the end of the day! I only have a couple pictures of myself with Brinkley that year, and we are sitting together on the floor in the family room. Brinkley looks more than a little perplexed in these photos too, kind of like his expression when he first glimpsed me as Big Bird, so when I used this picture in his scrapbook I captioned it with a little thought balloon above his head saying, "Uh-oh…Mommy is a jackass!" Talk about a good lesson in laughter!

Last but not least, a larger group of us also did a turn as the characters from the old television show "Hee-Haw"! We had a good number of the characters represented that year, including Grandpa Jones, Lulu, the farmer with the "BR-549" sign, the grouchy old woman with the rags in her hair who was always ironing and yelling at her husband, the redhead with braids, and I was the girl with the blonde bob and the bloodhound, Beauregard the Wonder Dog! For work purposes, I had a papier mache dog to represent Beauregard, but for our photos at home, I tied an orange bandana around Brinkley's neck and he sat next to me on the floor! That year we garnered a third place finish in the work competition and as usual, had a lot of fun in the process! This was one of the events that we always looked forward to participating in, and it was always enjoyable because I had such creative, fun-loving friends there!

In addition to being my sidekick when I dressed up in costume, Brinkley had a large array of costumes of his own! As previously stated, we discovered at an early age that Brinkley was pretty tolerant about costumes, and indeed, like my childhood dog, Taffy, pretty much anything that seemed to make us, his human family, happy! One of my favorite memories of Taffy is when I would have him lay on the upholstered wrought iron sofa on the sun porch, cover him with a blanket, and feed him water out of a baby bottle. Talk about a patient dog! And Brinkley was the same, always willing to endure whatever made us smile or laugh. I think the first kind of costume we ever tried on him was a headband, and he eventually came to have many of them. Even though Brinkley never liked the noise of fireworks on the fourth of July, I have some adorable pictures of him on the double rocker on the front porch, wearing a striped red, white and blue Uncle Sam hat on a headband and a reversible stars and stripes bandana custom-made for him by his Aunt Vicky, one of my dear friends from my Hobbico days. In subsequent years, Brinkley also had a Sassy Lassy headband for St. Patrick's Day, bunny ears and butterfly wings for Easter, and reindeer antlers for Christmas. The St. Patrick's Day I was between jobs was unseasonably warm and we took pictures of Brinkley on our back deck wearing the Sassy Lassy headband. We have a succession of pictures with him posing like the consummate professional model at first, and finally, at the end, laying with the headband between his big cocker spaniel paws after knocking it unceremoniously off his head! Later that evening at our annual St. Patrick's Day dinner, my Mom, Aunt Jean and I all took a turn wearing that headband, but I still think Brinkley wore it best! The bunny ears, too, produced a great series of photos, beginning with the ever-patient, long-suffering, please hurry up and take the picture so I can get out of these silly bunny ears poses, and one particularly funny shot where I think he was getting ready to sneeze, but it looks like he has his lip curled in a snarl, like a feral Easter bunny! I'm sure he must have been wondering, with his long, cocker spaniel ears, why he needed another pair of stand-up ears on top of his head! But Brinkley was a dog who lived to please, and when we were laughing he was happy too. Seems that we people could learn a lot from our canine companions when it comes to putting the happiness of others above our own. Must be just another of the multitude of reasons that God has paired us with the dog since the beginning of time.

Brinkley also had other memorable costume apparel that in turn produced memorable photos. Some items were sports-related, including a baseball cap. But most important was Brinkley's orange and blue Illini sweater, which I bought for him to wear the year that the Fighting Illini basketball team went all the way to the NCAA championship. In 2004-2005, the team revolved around a core group of five players, Deron Williams, Dee Brown, Luther Head, Roger Powell and James Augustine, and they not only played basketball at a phenomenal level, they inspired our community to new heights with their amazing teamwork and the way they worked together as a unit. I could try to describe the experience, but it really defies description. It was about so much more than winning basketball games! And while I enjoy watching basketball, I was over the moon about this season, this team, and this group of five incredible young men. So, when I watched the games on TV, I would get excited...okay, rabid...in my screaming and cheering for the team, especially during close games, and as usual in basketball, there were MANY close games! And Brinkley, ever the shy guy, did NOT like my screaming! I'm sure that he could not distinguish between my excited cheering of the team and the reason for most human shouting, which is typically done in anger. Not that we have ever done a lot of yelling at our house, but it was just too much for Brinkley, and he would get up and try to get out of the room, usually by scratching at the sliding patio doors in the family room. So I would try to tone it down, but it was really hard for me. And that's saying something, because no one who knows me outside of my immediate family would believe that I can get that loud! As a matter of fact, most people I know are always asking me to speak up because they can't hear my speaking voice! I'm really surprised that Brinkley survived the Arizona game, which came close to the end of championship play, because it seemed sure that we would not win that game, and I'm sure that anyone who listened to the game that night would vouch for me that it was a complete MIRACLE that we DID! From there we went all the way to the final game but lost to North Carolina in a match that I will always feel was unfairly officiated, but it just didn't matter. The team returned to a huge welcome in their hometown, and still hold a special place in all of our hearts for the joy they gave us that season. And I have some really cute pictures of Brinkley and me in our Illini gear, he in his orange and blue sweater and me in my Dee Brown #11 jersey, getting ready to watch the next game! And Brinkley, as usual, was forever faithful to watch with me, in spite of my inability to settle down!

In addition to his sports gear, Brinkley had some other, more comical, outfits, and seemed somehow to know how to pose in each one to make for a funnier picture. In one of the photos in his scrapbook, he is wearing a soda jerk hat and bandana, and he wouldn't even look at me in that picture! I captioned the photo with the phrase, "Hey, I'm no jerk…I'm a good sport!" And then there was the Sherlock Holmes hat. Even though Brinkley was still really young when we got him this cap, he somehow manages to look like a stodgy old fellow in it, full of consternation! And then, to top it all off, there was the Halloween after the movie "Pirates of the Caribbean" came out, when we got Brinkley a pirate hat, complete with long strands of black yarn for hair on both sides and a skull and crossbones bandana. As you can see from the photo at the beginning of this chapter, I'm not exaggerating when I say that Johnny Depp has NOTHING on Brinkley when it comes to portraying a sensitive pirate!

Besides the silly gear, Brinkley also had some clothes meant for practical purposes, including a number of sweaters to wear on winter walks, my favorite of which was dark red nubby fleece with a pair of leaping reindeer on it. He also had a beautiful light blue coat with natural fleece around the collar, and I have a photo of him sitting outside on the deck in that coat with his ears blowing in the wind, and I'm not kidding, he is as beautiful as CHRISTIE Brinkley, no pun intended! We also got him some boots, thinking that it would be wise to protect his little paddy paws from the cold and salt, but, like any dog, he never came to like them! At first, he walked around the family room with his legs all stiff, as if to say, "Mom, please take these off!" He did become accustomed to them in time and would wear them for walks on cold, snowy days, but the photo I have of him in the reindeer coat and boots says it all... "But Mom...all the other dogs will laugh at me!"

We were also able to find some great clothes for Brinkley on our yearly trips up to Michigan, since they have some great dog-themed shops there. Our favorite one also had the cleverest name, "Fuzzybutz Pet Bakery"! They sold T-shirts for pets and people with their logo printed on them, along with a very funny cartoon drawing of a little snaggle-toothed dog which posed the question "Do you have a fuzzy butt?" Of course we had to have T-shirts for Brinkley and for us, and had our pictures taken sitting on the steps of our deck, from the back so the shirts are readable! In Michigan, we also found perhaps the most fitting t-shirt that Brinkley ever possessed, since it proclaimed one of the great truths of Brinkley's life, "I love my Grandpa". Since little Murphy was Grandma's dog, and we had found him a bandana which stated this in no uncertain terms, it seemed only right to get this t-shirt for Brinkley. In addition, it was in Michigan that we found Brinkley's funniest ever outfit, a pair of surf shorts, or "jams" as the surfer dudes call them, for dogs, complete with a hole for the tail! It really is a good thing that Brinkley was such a good sport or he never would have tolerated those, but he just took them in stride, much like everything else that came into his life, both the good and the bad. Brinkley was a truly unflappable little dog, another characteristic we people could stand to learn a lot more about.

Perhaps that is why it didn't seem a stretch to dress Brinkley up in a pair of angel wings one Christmas, because that is what he truly was. The last year we had the privilege of having Brinkley with us, we found him a little charm to wear on his collar that read "99% angel". Nothing could have been closer to the truth. I always say that when he slipped the bounds of this earth, on his journey to Rainbow Bridge, he attained the additional 1%, although I really think he already possessed it while he was here with us.

Little Bits Of Joy – What Am I Doing Here With All These Dogs?

I have known my share of groomers, starting out with a very nice lady named Johnsy who worked at the vet's office where I went until my very special vet, Dr. Revis, started her own clinic. When Johnsy left the vet clinic we went on a quest for another groomer, which turned out to be quite an ordeal. I had some less than ideal experiences, including one that my family believes traumatized me for the rest of my life, because until that time I had not been fearful of loud noises, but after that I was. We finally found another very nice lady, Lois, in Monticello, and I went there for several years, but she had an injury on the day of one of my grooming appointments and when my family and Mommy arrived that day, we found no one at the shop. We understood what had happened but by that time I was in real need of a haircut, so on a whim, on the way home we stopped at Bark Avenue, a grooming salon close to our home. Mommy went in and spoke with the owner, Janice, and although she usually worked on shih tzus and smaller dogs, she agreed to schedule an appointment for me. At the time she had a helper working with her, and she did my hair the first couple times, but then she left the shop. However, by then Janice

53

had developed a soft spot for me (I have always had that effect on people!), so she agreed to continue taking care of me. Jan has a nice big window in her shop with a low bench in front of it, and that quickly became my favorite hangout so I could watch for Grandpa to come pulling in to pick me up after my haircut. The one thing I have never figured out is "What am I doing here with all these DOGS?" Since my family is all humans, I always feel a bit out of place at the groomer's and don't have much to do with the other dogs. Not that I am a snob, mind you, and there was a little shy guy named Chester whom I befriended. Jan told Mommy that he liked walking around with me, and I did think that was okay. Also, Mommy seemed delighted with the story about Chester and me, and like every good dog, I love to delight my Mommy!

What Brinkley Taught Me About...Coping With Change

I am not a person who adapts easily to change. At least it has never come naturally to me, perhaps because of the way I was brought up. I have lived my entire life within an approximate two-mile radius. My parents lived on Southwood Drive when I was born and we lived there until I was four years old. At that time, we had a new home built on Brookshire East and relocated just a couple minutes away from our current home. I lived there with my family until the age of twenty-four, when I got married. As an only child, I have always had an extremely close relationship with my parents, so this was never an issue. We are a very tightly knit little unit of three. My husband, too, fits nicely into this structure, so we also operate well as a unit of four when we are all together. This is a very important factor, as you will see as we look further into the future.

My husband, Tim, and I have led similar lives in some respects, and having lived all of our lives within a small radius is one of them. Tim was also born in town and has lived here all his life. Neither of us even ventured away for college. We both attended Parkland Community College here in town, Tim with plans of transferring to the

University of Illinois in mechanical engineering, and me to obtain an Associate's Degree in Visual Arts, which at the time I was entering the field was just as likely to get you a job as the more expensive route of attending a four-year college. But prior to transferring to the U of I, Tim found a job with Wandell's, a local nursery and landscaping company, which eventually led to him becoming the head grower and greenhouse manager for Prairie Gardens, where he worked for thirty-seven years. I began working at Prairie Gardens part time at the age of seventeen, my senior year in high school, as a sign maker. Back then, I hand-lettered all the signs for the store, in marker for the inside of the store and in paint for the outside. Hand lettering has always been a passion of mine; I also do calligraphy, so this was an ideal fit for me. This is where Tim and I met and began dating. After we had been dating for several years and it looked as though we might be married someday, we made the decision that I should look for a job elsewhere so we would not both be employed by the same company if that should happen. I only had a couple interviews before being hired on the spot at a local radio control model company, Tower Hobbies, which had been launched by a married couple, Bruce and Jeri Holecek. I had worked at Prairie Gardens for five years, gone from part time while attending college to full time once I graduated, and assumed the additional responsibilities of laying out the newspaper ads. I was primed and ready to begin my new adventure as a graphic artist in the advertising department at Tower Hobbies!

I began my new career with Tower Hobbies in June of 1985, and Tim and I got married in September of 1987. Tim is older and already had a house, but we bought a new home together in order to have a fresh start as newlyweds. Our new house was on Coventry Drive, in Maynard Lake subdivision, and was only a couple miles from where I had grown up on Brookshire East. I was happy that Tim was established in his job at Prairie Gardens and not likely to have to relocate, because of my closeness with my family. Tim's parents had also lived in Urbana for many years, having moved to their current home on Main Street when Tim was five years old. Tim also has an older brother, Steve, and he lives locally as well. We planned to stay in our current jobs until retirement, and our current home into old age. However, after we had lived on Coventry for about eight years, the developer of the subdivision began to expand the neighborhood, with plans to build additional homes right behind our house. When we moved in, we liked that it was all empty fields behind the house, with Interstate 57 out beyond that. We didn't want to have another house right behind ours, especially since our house was set up high on the lot with a deck leading out into the back yard, so we would be looking right out of our large kitchen windows and over our five-foot back fence into the back windows of our new neighbors' house. Although we loved our home, we began to look for another one.

We were on a cruise with Tim's company in March of 1995 when my parents informed us that they were anxious for us to return because the house next door to theirs had just gone up for sale! It was a big, colonial-style two-story with a swimming pool and six bedrooms, which was really a lot more house than we needed since we had no children, but it was all about location! The day we returned, we made arrangements with Liz, the realtor we had been working with, to see the house. We made an offer the same day, but the speed of the deal gave the current owner cold feet, and she did not accept immediately. Hannah was in the process of getting a divorce, and decided to hole herself up in the house and not allow further access. Eventually we had to get Wendy, our lawyer, involved. Wendy is a wonderful person and a force to be reckoned with, and having her in our corner proved to be invaluable in securing our new house. At one point in the negotiation process, she pulled us out of the room and asked us, "How bad do you want this house?" When we responded, "We really want this house!" she said, "Then we'll get it for you!" And she did…at the closing for the house, Hannah was down the hall at the courtroom getting remarried, and that sealed the deal…the house was now officially ours and Hannah was on her way to being evicted!

The change of houses was unexpected, but welcome, as we were now next door to my Mom and Dad. At that time we had our first cocker spaniel together, Murphy, who was about six years old when we moved in. He quickly became my Mom's little gardening buddy, and loved to go next door and spend the days in the yard with her while Tim and I were at work. I still believe that Mom had the closest relationship with Murphy, and she became his main caretaker when he became sickly in his old age. Murphy had a kerchief that said "I'm Grandma's Dog" and he really was. The two of them absolutely adored one another and spent many happy hours together. And we all enjoyed kicking back on the front porch or back decks of our houses when time allowed. It was great being so close that all we had to do was step outside to spend some time together!

Tim continued working at Prairie Gardens as he had always planned, and we were like family with the owner and all the members of management and their spouses. I continued in my career as well, and shortly after I started working there, Tower Hobbies merged with Great Planes Model Manufacturing to become Hobbico, now encompassing both the retail and wholesale branches of the radio control market. Around the same time that Murphy left us and Brinkley joined our family in 2001, I had worked my way up to middle management by becoming the supervisor of the retail division, working for my former college professor, Julie, who was also a great friend of mine. My staff was composed of friends of many years when we were all artists together. My evaluations and raises were all exceptional, and while at times I would wonder if there was something more to life than radio control models, I loved my job and everyone I worked with. I had no plans of ever leaving. Then came Wednesday, December 17th, 2008.

December 17th is Tim's birthday, but this year had been a tough one for our family. My Aunt Jean had been through some major trials with her health beginning in the fall of 2006, and had been recently hospitalized, still not out of the woods. Tim's mom had a heart attack and bypass surgery and had just been released from the hospital and a couple weeks' rehab at the nursing home. Tim was at the hospital with his Dad that day as he was having his current pacemaker replaced. It was the end of the day when Julie summoned me to the conference room. When Julie closed the door behind me, Chris, our vice president of advertising, asked me to take a seat. She wasted no time explaining and made no apology for why I was there. The company was downsizing and it had been decided to terminate my position. I would be leaving for the last time that very day. I sat for a moment in stunned silence before catching my breath and starting to cry. Julie was sitting next to me, crying too, and took my hand and gave it a squeeze. I asked Chris if I could take some other job within the company, even in the warehouse, but the answer was a flat no. After ensuring that all of my staff had left for the evening, I was escorted back to my desk to pack up my belongings, and then out to my car by a male co-worker who helped me carry my boxes. At least he expressed his condolences for my situation. It was the only expression of sympathy I received on my way out. Once I was in the car, I called Tim to tell him what had happened. He was still in the recovery room with his Dad at the hospital and was unable to come right home, but he did immediately call my parents. They were on their way home at the time and met me at the back door as soon as I arrived. Thank God that Brinkley and my family were there for me that first evening. I don't know how I could have processed the shock of what had just happened to me after twenty-three years with the same company without their love and support.

God's timing, however, was perfect that day, although at the time it just seemed ironic. I had chosen a brand new sweatshirt I had ordered from the Quacker Factory to wear that day, which said "Angels Don't Worry...They Believe". It took me a mighty long time to make the journey through worry to belief, but now I see that the words on my sweatshirt that day are true. But as I said, it has taken a journey...

My first day of unemployment found us without health insurance, as I had been the insurance carrier for both Tim and myself. I had the option of continuing coverage via COBRA at three times the cost it had been when I was employed, but this seemed absurd since I now had no income, so Tim contacted Grace, the human resources manager at Prairie Gardens, and bless her heart, she was able to get us covered through Prairie Gardens that same day. That worry was behind us. Now I faced the very intimidating task of finding a new job after being so long with one company. Since I had been a supervisor for the last seven years of my employment, I had never been trained on the new computer programs the artists were using, so it seemed unlikely that I would even be able to secure a job in my current field. I was going to have to sail an uncharted course, me, the person who had never liked dealing with change.

On Friday, I called the unemployment office and was on hold for something like an hour and a half. The last quarter of 2008 is well-known as a period of mass layoffs, and obviously I was not the only person out of work a week before Christmas. However, when at last someone picked up the phone, God's selection of the person I got on the line again proved His sovereignty. Stanley was his name, and he was the most compassionate person I can imagine speaking to in that situation. I never would have expected this, especially from someone working at a government agency, but he told me that the same thing had happened to him after years of service at the company he once worked for. He helped me understand what I needed to do to begin receiving my unemployment benefits right away, assured me that I would be successful in finding another job, and even gave me his back line in case I needed any further assistance to save me from being on death hold again. And so I thanked God again for Stanley and his overwhelming kindnesses to me when I needed them so much.

Thus began my search for a new job and my efforts to reinvent myself at the age of forty-five. I am so grateful that I was born again and rededicated my life to the Lord in February of 1997, because He was my anchor throughout the whole long ordeal that followed my termination from my job. Now that I had time on my hands between job searching and soul searching, I spent much time in prayer, mainly with little Brinkley right by my side in the big chair in the family room. Every morning I would get the computer out and begin my job search for the day, both in order to find a new job and to fulfill my responsibilities to the unemployment office and receive my benefits each week. I was required to fill out a sheet with at least five companies per week where I had sought employment, and had to call in each week to certify for benefits. Brinkley was there for me every day as I searched for my next opportunity and to seek God's will for my life from here on. His quiet presence beside me helped me ground my anxious spirit during those uneasy days in a way I could never adequately describe, but which needs no explanation for anyone who has ever traversed troubled times with a beloved dog as their companion.

God's perfect timing during this period of my life was also evident in the events that my family was experiencing at the time. In February of 2009, my Aunt had to make the transition from hospitalization following surgery to a stay in an extended care facility for rehab, and the day she was released from the hospital, my Mom had the flu. I was able to meet my Aunt at the rehab facility after she was transported there and help her get settled in her new room, then follow up with her the next day as my Mom was still sick. This really helped ease my Mom's mind that I was able to step into the gap and take care of things for Aunt Jean when she was unable to do so herself, and I still believe that it was part of God's master plan for my period of unemployment that I was available to help with things like this when my assistance was needed.

While I was out of work, I did find part-time employment at Curves, where I went at that time to work out. Mom and I had joined several years before and had become great friends with the owner and all the ladies who worked there. Darby was a wonderful, supportive friend, and had even hosted an event at Curves when I published my first book of inspirational poetry, so she agreed to train me to be a circuit coach. Norma and the other trainers also worked with me, and in early Spring I began working part-time there. I had never worked with the public, so this was really out of the box for me, but I discovered that I loved it! I am a born encourager of others, even though I have had my struggles with believing in myself over the years, so it came naturally for me to walk the circuit with the ladies on the machines, talking with them and providing guidance and an encouraging word. I really loved this job and would have been happy to stay there, but I needed a full-time job with benefits. So around the same time I was really hitting my stride at Curves, I found a job listing for an assistant editor at Human Kinetics, a local publisher of books and journals. The ad specified a need for someone who was detail-oriented and highly accurate, both traits of mine, and I was very excited to receive a call to interview for the journals department after filling out an application. I was even more excited to see the facility when I interviewed...the building was stunning, more like a beautiful home than an office, with each editor having their own private office with their name on the door, which could be decorated to suit one's own personal style. And then there were the grounds where the facility was located! It was not in the best part of town, but you would never have known it, because it was surrounded with the most beautiful landscaping, winding paths bordered with flowers and trees for walking, and an outdoor eating area off the full-service cafeteria, complete with tables with umbrellas and a waterfall for ambiance! I was quite literally blown away. I wanted to work there so badly that I even tried to put it out of my head that when I saw samples of the journals that I would be editing, I found them to be very dry. I was just sure that I would be happy there no matter what I was doing!

It was April 1st of 2009, my 46th birthday, when I found out that I had not been selected for the job of journals managing editor at Human Kinetics. I was disappointed, but not as crushed as I thought I would be, because I was told that there might be another opportunity in the books department. It was then that I was able to admit that I had found the journals pretty boring, and that I was actually happier about the prospect of working on books. I did some preliminary testing prior to the second interview and was actually considered for the position of developmental editor, a step up the ladder from the assistant editor position I was to interview for, but at that point it was decided to proceed with the interview for the assistant editor position. Lynn, the hiring manager for the position, was very impressed with my skills and I immediately liked her and everyone I met at my interview, and it wasn't more than a couple days later that I received a phone call offering me the job, along with an increase in the hourly pay due to my previous experience in proofreading! I was over the moon! I was going to be an assistant editor of scientific, technical and medical books for college level students at the most beautiful facility I had ever seen!

I started my new career in editing on June 29th of 2009, working closely with the other assistant editors who took me under their wings by training me and inviting me to lunch in the fabulous cafeteria. Even the food was extraordinary at this wonderful new job, and I felt right at home with the other assistant editors even though they were all young enough to be my daughters! I was paired up with a very sweet young lady named Rachel, and we shared an office for several months until an office became available for me to have my own. Rachel would come and get me for breaks and lunch and while I loved her, I found that I always felt nervous on my new job. I figured it would pass, but the feelings persisted. I was always working through breaks and staying late to try and keep up, and bringing work home to work off the clock. We didn't use a time clock but were on the honor system of just writing down our times, so I often fudged on mine in order to look like I was achieving my work in less time than it was really taking. Then Lynn began to question whether I could do specific tasks in time frames that I felt were unrealistic in terms of the high degree of accuracy expected in our work. I was honest with her about how much time I felt I needed in order to do a good job, but she was not happy with my estimates. I did manage to dodge a corporate downsize of about thirty people around Christmas in 2009 (exactly a year after the Christmas downsize of 2008 that had claimed my job at Hobbico), but by February of 2010 I was on the ropes again. I was given ninety days to turn things around or to once again face looking for another job. Also, and again completely out of the blue, Tim was having issues at his job! In December, when my job was temporarily spared, he was called in shortly after a glowing evaluation and told that he was not doing his job and was being demoted. He would be losing his title and one third of his pay. It was impossible for us to believe that the boss we had always thought of as family would do such a thing.

I was pretty sure by the time I was given the ultimatum that I could not deliver the high quality work that my authors expected in the time frame that Lynn expected, and in spite of the newspaper ad to which my skills seemed so well suited, that this job was not a good fit for me. I was a bundle of nerves sitting all alone in my office each day, and by the time lunch rolled around, my stomach was twisted in knots so that I could not even enjoy the company of the other assistant editors or the wonderful food served in the beautiful cafeteria. I did feel that the authors I was working with appreciated the painstaking care I was taking with their work, and that Chris and Judy, the two developmental editors I worked with, felt that I was doing a good job. But during my ninety-day probationary period, I had to meet with Lynn every two weeks to go over my progress, or lack thereof, and that did nothing but exacerbate my anxiety issues and lack of self-esteem. Lynn would even tell me that I lacked self-confidence, and that she couldn't give that to me, seemingly without realizing that those very meetings were only aggravating the problem! Then, God's timing came into play again, this time in the form of an injury that Brinkley suffered to his left back leg. Brinkley had always had issues with his back legs, starting even before he turned one year old, and that spring he hurt the left knee and would require a double surgery. It was right about at the end of my probationary period at Human Kinetics, and I was already sure that they would not be keeping me on.

While I do think that Human Kinetics lost a good editor when they let me go, I do agree that the job was not a good fit for me, and I am grateful that at least with them I knew where I stood prior to being let go. They were also gracious enough to allow me to work two extra weeks, which allowed me to finish my fifth book and send it to the printer on my last day. And as I mentioned, God's timing was obvious once again. My last day at Human Kinetics was on May 7th, 2010, the day of Brinkley's knee surgery, so I would be home to care for him during his recovery, which would be extensive. Also, the sum I received as severance pay from Human Kinetics was the exact amount needed to cover the costs of Brinkley's surgery. Only God could have orchestrated such a remarkable double miracle.

Brinkley stayed the night at the Animal Emergency Clinic and came home on Saturday, May 8th. It was time for me to be there for him as he had always been for me. He came home with his little knee all stitched up, and very limited mobility. For many weeks he was not to be off a very short leash, and allowed absolutely no running or jumping, since the knee would have to have additional surgery if he should reinjure it. I was so glad we had not opted to have the surgery when he was a puppy, since I could not imagine trying to keep a puppy that still! So, while Brinkley recovered, I resumed my job search, this time collecting unemployment from Human Kinetics, tracking my weekly applications and focusing my search on Carle Hospital, whom I had always felt would be a good employer.

In looking for jobs at Carle, I met a highly dedicated lady in Human Resources, LouAnn. I was advised by a friend at church that if I wanted to be seriously considered for any job at Carle that I should go through HR, and that was advice wisely heeded. LouAnn met with me to go over my job skills and took a personal interest in getting interviews for me. She worked tirelessly, sometimes calling me late in the evening as she was still at work. I interviewed a total of seven times prior to being hired, three times in the psychology department, first for phones and twice for check out. I would have been hired for the second position except that a current Carle employee who had been on staff for over twenty years applied at the last minute! I would have taken that news hard, especially since the location was just down the street from our house, but just two weeks later I was called to interview in the orthopedics department, which was also just down the street but even closer to home! I was on vacation in Michigan when I got the call to interview, but made arrangements with Dana to come in as soon as we returned. I did so, got the tour of the department and met everyone, and felt right at home immediately. Imagine my delight when I got a call from LouAnn shortly after my interview, stating that Dana had called her to say that she "just loved me"! I had interviewed for part-time in podiatry, but when the offer came in a couple days later, I was offered that job or the choice of a full-time position with hand surgery! Since full time was what I really needed, along with the better benefits it offered, I accepted the newly open position. I worked in the orthopedics department for almost six years before transferring to the allergy department in June of 2016, and I finally realized that, indeed, there is more to life than radio control models, since now I am helping people on a daily basis and have the opportunity to shine the light of Christ in doing so.

One year after my job change to Carle, Tim got his courage up and found a new job as the manager of the outdoor lawn and garden department at our local Lowe's home improvement store. He has brought a new level of quality and knowledge to his department, along with a loyal following of former customers from Prairie Gardens who have sought him out and followed him there. He can't believe he didn't make the move sooner and is so happy to have a life outside of work now, which with his former schedule he didn't have time to enjoy. Funny how the changes we were so resistant to have now transformed our lives, and even our marriage.

And through it all, this marvelous, understanding little dog named Brinkley was there for us, buoying up our spirits, lending an always-listening ear, and helping us learn to roll with the changes. Somehow, through that all-knowing gaze, he was able to see into our souls and to convey to us that everything would come out all right. He must have had a direct line to God to know that, but then, dogs, in their purity of heart, surely have exactly that.

Little Bits Of Joy – Sing Along With Sheila

I am not a dog who does much vocalizing. Occasionally, when I am on my front porch, someone has the audacity to go jogging by, and then I bark. I do not understand running. I am always wondering what they are running from. I guess I got that perception from Mommy, who also does not understand running. Many times I have heard Mommy say that the only good reason for running is if someone is chasing you. So when I see those joggers going by on the sidewalk, and no one in hot pursuit, it just makes no sense to me. But I digress. The point is, I am not much of a barker, howler, or whiner. Well, unless I catch sight of my Grandpa out in the yard. Then when I get his attention and he starts on his way over to pet my head, I DO whine for him. He is someone super special! I should note one other exception: I have a favorite song, and if I did karaoke, I would choose this one. It is Sheila Walsh's version of the wonderful old hymn, "How Great Thou Art". Mommy likes to listen to our local Christian radio station, Great News Radio, and whenever I hear that song, my ears perk up. Sheila has a really pretty, clear, high soprano voice, and when she gets into the middle of the song, I join in with little barks for emphasis. And by the time she wraps things up, I am in full-out howling mode, singing along with Sheila! Mommy and Daddy leave the radio on for me some nights; I sleep downstairs in my crate and they go upstairs to bed. They use a baby monitor so they will know if I need anything in the night, and Mommy can hear me if I start scratching at the crate. Well, sometimes they hear me howling and wonder what is up…it isn't storming…maybe I have gotten sick in my crate. Then when Mommy comes down to check on me, Sheila is just finishing her song and I am singing along. And I tell you what; nothing delights Mommy like me singing along with that favorite old hymn…even in the middle of the night that will make her smile! And as every good dog knows, making our humans smile brings us a smile as well!

What Brinkley Taught Me About...Overcoming The Blues

I won't lie...I have had my struggles with depression, some of them justified and others not so much, just that, like many folks, I have a dark side which occasionally rears its ugly head and causes me to feel sorry for myself. I had a happy childhood with a stable family background so it was never an issue back then, but as I entered my teens I began to experience some negative thought patterns emerging from time to time. I don't find this unusual, since the teen years are perhaps the most ripe for upheaval of any time period in life, and I had some additional circumstances that fueled the fire when it came to depression. For one, I have always been a good listener, and in being that kind of rare person, you sometimes (okay, often) attract troubled friends who need someone to talk to. I remember as far back as junior high having a friend with suicidal tendencies whom I had to persuade that there were many people who cared about her and that she should not feel as if there was no one who felt that way. It seemed that there was always at least one person in my life at any given time who was in a state of depression themselves, so I was always aware of the presence of depression around me. In addition, I have always been a perfectionist, with all of the baggage that comes with that personality type, so I was often discouraged with myself when I came up short of perfection, which is, of course, all the time. I have pretty much always been my own worst enemy and harder on myself than anyone else. So I had a few rough years in my teens, although I wouldn't say that was when I had my first real bout with depression, just more of a series of rollercoaster highs and lows as often experienced during that time of life.

Although this book is primarily about Brinkley, my third cocker spaniel, I would be remiss if I did not address the truth that ALL of my dogs have taught and helped me a great deal, especially in this area of overcoming the blues. Since I have always been prone to bouts with depression, I am all the more certain that it has been God's will that I have had a dog throughout most of my life. I begged my parents for a dog for what seemed like an eternity, to a child at least, before they allowed Taffy to join our family when I was nine years old. We all agree now that it was the best $35 we ever spent. Yes, Taffy was only $35 for seventeen years of pure joy! Where else can you get a deal like that? Adopting him into our family was one of the best decisions we ever made. And in looking back on my teen years, I don't know how I would have made it through without Taffy. Taffy was a sunny optimist, always right there beside me...my constant companion, sidekick and shadow. I referred to him as my "little brother", and since I had no human siblings he was also my confidante. And perhaps dogs make the BEST confidantes, because you know when you tell a dog your deepest secrets, they're never going to run and tell someone else if they decide it would be beneficial to do so, or slip up and tell something they're not supposed to reveal. So, while I was basically always a "good kid", I did go through some rough times between the ages of thirteen and seventeen, and Taffy was always there for me. And I will be forever grateful for my very best childhood friend. I can't wait to see him again one day!

My first real encounter with depression was to come later on, after about ten years of marriage. I doubt very much that this is uncommon either, or that most married couples have experienced trials like this at some point in time, but I got into a real extended funk over my real and imagined issues, to the point that I am surprised that our marriage survived it. I was raised in a Christian home and had always attended church regularly until I got into my late teens and lost interest in my faith. I stopped going to church and fell away from my relationship with God, returning only when I became engaged to be married and wished to do so in the church where I had been raised and where my parents still faithfully attended. The pastor at that time was a deeply devout man and required that couples go through several counseling sessions prior to their wedding date, so Tim and I obliged. While I found myself a bit disgruntled at times with the advice I was given, I did feel that we learned a lot from our sessions, but still did not feel any pull back to my former faith. We married in the church but did not resume attendance. We continued in this manner until I hit my rough spot at the age of 33, desperately seeking the happiness and joy in life that I felt I had utterly lost.

In my quest to rediscover happiness, I tried a number of different avenues, all of them destructive, all of them failures. Then in February of 1997, I discovered that I had endometriosis and had to have surgery. Tim and I had been trying unsuccessfully to have a child for the past three years; perhaps this was the reason we could not do so. At any rate, I had the surgery and took the next week off work to rest, while my Mom babied me with wonderful home-cooked meals each night. When I returned to work, my Dad drove me for the first week so I would not have to walk far in the cold. It was on one such occasion that my life turned around, or perhaps it would be more accurate to say, upside down.

When Dad picked me up after work on one of those evenings that week, he had a CD of the Gaither Vocal Band on in his vehicle. The song that was playing was "Mountains of Mercy". In what had to be a total intervention by the Holy Spirit, the lyric to that song grabbed my attention and held it fast. Suddenly I knew what was missing in my life… my faith and my relationship with God! I have to admit, it wasn't a gung-ho conversion that I can be totally proud of, casting my life fully before Him in complete trust and abandon to my own will…it was more of a "Well, I've tried everything else in order to find happiness again…might as well try God". But believe it or not, this was enough for Him! It was a lot like the story of the Prodigal Son, where the father comes running to the errant son, throwing his arms around him, even as undeserving as he was. That was the way I felt…just an inexpressible, overwhelming sense of love pouring forth from my Heavenly Father, even after the way I had lived my own life and ignored His will for me for all of those years. I consider February 22nd, 1997, as my spiritual birthday, the day I made the best decision of my life, to return to a right relationship with my Lord and Savior, Jesus Christ.

To continue acknowledging the contributions that all of my dogs have made to my well-being, I give my second cocker spaniel, Murphy, full credit for seeing me through this difficult time in my life. When Tim and I got married, Taffy stayed with my Mom and Dad since that was the only home he had ever known, and Tim also had a fairly elderly cat. We couldn't see any way to merge the two into one home at their ages, and it wasn't any problem to see Taffy often since we all lived in the same town and saw each other frequently. Taffy and Charlie, Tim's cat, passed away within about three months of one another, two years after Tim and I got married. Talk about a rough time for all of us…we just felt lost without our beloved pets of so many years. So in October of 1989, Tim went on a search for cocker spaniel puppies and located a litter on a farm near Springfield, Illinois who were ready for adoption. We arranged to go and see them on Sunday, October 8th, with the option of selecting whichever of the four males we wanted. However, when we arrived, there was a lady with a little girl who had arrived ahead of us. We watched as the puppies' mother ran across the yard with three little buff babies and one red trying to keep up! It was a challenge with their plump, well-fed little tummies practically dragging the ground! I will remember it always! Well, Tim and I fell in love with the little redhead, but tried to downplay it for fear that the little girl would want whichever puppy we showed an interest in, and our plan worked. The little girl, who really didn't seem as interested as her mother in a puppy, chose one of the buff puppies, and we were soon on our way home with our first little redhead! And little Murphy proved to be just as much of a joy to our entire family as Taffy had been. He began life with us when we lived on Coventry Drive, and then made the move to Brookshire when he was six years old. This move proved to be wonderful for him, as he was now living next door to his grandparents and was able to go next door on nice days and help his Grandma in her garden. Murphy was Grandma's dog from that time forward, and she really had the closest bond with him, even stepping in to be his caretaker the last year of his life when he needed more help. I feel regretful at times that I was not there for Murphy as much as I believe I should have been, mainly because of the powerful pull of my negative emotions throughout this period of his lifetime. But my love for him and desire to keep our family together probably had more influence than anything else could have at that time in terms of keeping me in my marriage and making me work things out instead of just giving up and moving on. And for that I will always owe Murphy an eternal debt of gratitude, because in the midst of finding my way through all that I also rediscovered my long-lost relationship with the Lord!

After rededicating my life to Christ, I tried some different avenues with my various talents and gifts to "get the word out" about the Lord and His goodness to us. My first venture was "Grandma's Garden", an idea that I came up with to honor my maternal grandmother. She was undoubtedly the strongest influence in my life when it came to all things of a spiritual nature, and in spite of her very petite physical presence, she was a mighty prayer warrior and witness for our Lord. The premise of "Grandma's Garden" was to create framed art featuring my talents in calligraphy in combination with bits of spiritual poetry, quotes, or scriptures along with cutouts from greeting cards, wrapping paper, or other sources for visual accent. These pieces were popular with friends and family members, and I even landed an opportunity to do a craft show as the featured artist at a shop in Tuscola. At the time, my Mom was making handcrafted wreaths with dolls and angels in them, and they were absolutely beautiful, so she agreed to display her items in a booth as part of the street festival that day. Unfortunately, our efforts seemed in vain, and for all the nice compliments we received, we made only a few sales. We ended up using the items we had made for Christmas gifts that year, and everyone who got them seemed very pleased with them, but I never could understand why this venture, which I had covered with so much prayer and felt so led by the Lord to pursue, wasn't more successful.

Also since my rebirth, I returned to my interest in writing poetry, this time making the decision to use this gift that God had given me early in life for His glory. I started writing in grade school, and had a teacher in the fifth grade who really encouraged me in this by helping me to assemble a book with all of my poems in it, along with a laminated cover for which I had drawn the artwork. My love for writing continued through high school, at that point in my life serving as a much-needed outlet and "safety valve" for many of the strong emotions I was feeling. I also had a couple teachers, one in junior high and another in high school, who were very supportive and great encouragers in regards to my writing. When I started college, my focus shifted to all art as I worked toward my Associate's Degree in Visual Arts, so I stopped writing. For me, writing has always required time spent in solitude, getting in touch with my thoughts, with the natural world around me, and waiting for inspiration. Now that I had this new and wonderful relationship with Jesus, I committed this gift to Him, and in return He inspired many new poems about spiritual topics. I began to share these with family and friends, writing an annual poem for Christmas and Easter, along with the many other poems that I felt that Christ was writing "through" me...that He was actually the author of these works and that I was merely His instrument for putting them down on paper. I had a friend at work who kept insisting that I should publish my work, and she really was quite relentless in pressing me to do so. I began to do some research on how to get my work published and came up with the name of a publisher in Bloomington, Indiana, AuthorHouse, so I contacted them. I found a very helpful representative there to guide me through the steps to getting my work published. I even found several ways to incorporate my visual work into the book, the first of which was shooting the front cover photo of a beautiful sunrise. As a teen I often got up and went outside at dawn when I was planning to write, to listen to the lilting trill of robins as they anticipated the sunrise. I also designed scrapbook pages as dividers for each section of the book, then photographed them for use in black and white in the interior of the book. In one of those photos, for the section of miscellaneous poems at the end of the book, little Brinkley was laying right next to me, and although he does not appear in the picture, he was watching me write as he often did! I published my book, "Inspired By The Master", in July of 2008. It was a very exciting venture, and again met with success among family and friends. In all I sold somewhere around 300 copies, but had limited success with book signings. I had one at Curves where I worked out at the time. Darby, the owner of the location where I went was so gracious that she arranged the event for me, setting me up at a lovely table complete with a flower arrangement she bought for me in congratulations for my achievement. I also had a signing at a local bookstore, but made only a few sales at either venue. However, I did succeed in getting much of my work read on our local Christian radio station, Great News Radio, and Mark and Carrie, the founders of that station, were very supportive in getting my poetry out there to their listeners. In spite of the limited outreach for my book, I am eternally grateful to everyone who tried to help me along the way. And I know it's true that we can never fully know the impact of our work for Christ while we are residents of this world, so I am hopeful that my poetry has had a wider scope of influence than I am aware of. After all, who knows how many radio listeners may have heard my poetry on Great News Radio and perhaps come into a right relationship with the Lord? Time will eventually tell! And one fine day, when I meet my Maker in Heaven, I will meet them too! What a glorious day that will be!

I then turned my interests to photography, a hobby I have always been in love with, and which had been part of my field of studies as a graphic artist. When I attended Parkland College to earn my Associate's Degree in Visual Arts, I took photography courses, where I learned all about operating a manual camera, shooting black and white photos, developing the film in a canister, and working with an enlarger to expose the negatives onto photo paper and process the photos with a series of chemicals in trays. I know I am dating myself here, but that is how it used to be done before the age of digital photography! And it was fun! So fun, in fact, that when my husband and I were first married, I got him interested enough to set up a darkroom in the attic of our first home, and we both thoroughly enjoyed working on photos up there. We also invested in a color enlarger and planned to pursue color processing, but never got it off the ground. But back to how I reignited my interest in photography... By this time I had a digital camera, although still the type I could have control over, much like the traditional manual camera I had worked with while at Parkland. As I remember it, the year I began taking a lot of pictures again we had a very early spring, and the crocuses, daffodils, and hyacinths were in full bloom in early March. And while that happens from time to time, we always get a cold snap shortly after they come out, and they get ruined soon after blooming. But this spring was different. It got warm and stayed warm, and little Brinkley and I were out for walks every day. And I brought my camera along, because the flowers were simply marvelous! So I had a wealth of pretty photographs. And then I had an idea for what I could do with them. Since one of my spiritual gifts has always been to encourage others, I came up with the idea to produce a line of greeting cards, called Bright Spots, with the slogan of "encourage...uplift...inspire". I got blank greeting cards and used my photos on the front, with my company name and slogan, along with a little drawing of half a sunburst, on the back. The inside would either be left blank for the person sending the card to write their own note or message, or could be inscribed with calligraphy or script with a message of the sender's choice. I developed a scrapbook of all my photos, adding new ones as I took them, and offered the cards for individual sale or in packs of six for the price of five, tied with a ribbon. I also used the photos in framed art, much as I had with Grandma's Garden. Again, this venture met with limited success, and again, mostly among family and friends. I made some sales just by sending the cards out…people often complimented me on them and when I had the opportunity, I would tell them that I also offered the cards for sale. Some people would be interested enough to look through the scrapbook, and I did sell some cards and framed art that way. I also did a second event with Great News Radio (the first was a book signing for "Inspired By The Master") at the Olive Garden restaurant, along with a holiday craft show at Carle hospital and sold some that way, but did not achieve the results I was hoping for.

Throughout all the ups and downs of my personal ventures in writing my book of poetry and creating the greeting cards and art for Bright Spots, Brinkley was my constant companion, sitting beside me as I wrote, going on outings with me to shoot photos, and boosting my morale with his cheery little spirit when things didn't go as planned. I guess I have always wondered why none of my ideas, while at the time, and even as I think of them now, have met with greater success. I have truly felt that each idea was given to me by the Lord, and was anointed by Him. But I do believe that even through these seemingly small ventures, God is teaching me. He has gifted me with my wonderful dogs to see me through, and in their quiet presence beside me during good times and bad, they have taught me far more than words of wisdom, no matter how eloquent or well-intentioned, from any fellow human being could have. And perhaps the lessons I have learned in humility have been even more valuable than had I been overwhelmingly successful. After all, humility is a lesson best learned from our dogs as well. Because just as our dogs are so effortlessly humble before their masters (us), we must learn to be (often far less effortlessly) humble before our Master (God). So perhaps in all of this, God has been teaching me to be more humble before Him, and to trust that his plan for me, whether through the ease of success or the challenge of trials, is perfect. And that lesson, unlike earthly successes, reaps an eternal reward. One I'm certain that our dogs, in the beautiful simplicity of their souls, understand far better than we.

Little Bits Of Joy – Joyrides In The Eddie...& Other Delights!

It's no secret...I adore my Grandma and Grandpa, and they seem to feel the same way about me! They never treat me like a dog, but instead like the treasured grandchild they never had. We have lots of fun together no matter what we are doing, but I have several favorite activities to do with my grandparents. One of them is walkies with Grandpa! When I was younger we went on walkies together a lot since Mommy and Daddy were always away at work during the day. And since taking a walk is one of my favorite activities, and Grandpa is one of my favorite people (so much so that I have a T-shirt that Mommy bought for me in Michigan that says, unashamedly, "I Love My Grandpa"), it is the perfect combination! And of course, I LOVE it when Mommy and Daddy invite Grandma and Grandpa over to sit on the front porch with them! In the summer, they often get these delicious frozen drinks called icy mochas from Panera, and when they get finished I get to lick the straw...YUM! And recently, now that I am older, they have started taking me for "joyrides in the Eddie". Grandpa has a Ford Explorer, the Eddie Bauer edition, and has always driven me to the groomer and I really get a kick out of riding in the car. So,

Grandma had the idea that they could pick me up and just take me for a ride every once in a while, and since Grandma has always enjoyed riding around the nicer neighborhoods in town and looking at all the big, fancy houses, that is what we do. I like to sit on her lap or right next to her in the back seat and look out the window at the pretty houses. And even though Grandpa gets the most vocal response from me when I see him (he is the only person that makes me whine, or "fuss", as Mommy says), there is no doubt that I love my Grammy too! I consider myself the luckiest dog on earth that I get to live right next door to my grandparents and be a "shared dog", because I love every member of my family the same, but for different reasons. And because I am a very good dog, I know what every member of my family needs from me and take great pleasure in providing those things for each of them!

What Brinkley Taught Me About...Patience in Affliction

If there's one thing Brinkley taught me better than any of my other dogs, it is the grace of patience in the face of affliction. I say this because Brinkley had to deal with more difficulties than any of my other boys. Taffy, my childhood buddy and "little brother" was a very healthy dog. He never even had to go to the vet's office for yearly shots because his vet lived across the street from us and I babysat for his four children, so when it was time for a rabies booster Bill just came over and did it at our house. He did have an issue at the age of fifteen that required minor surgery, and then he lived to be just a month shy of seventeen, but other than that he never required any medical attention. Murphy, my first baby with Tim, had also done pretty well other than a knee surgery around the age of seven or eight, and then he was in good health until his stroke when he was eleven. The stroke gave him a little tilty head which was really quite adorable, but after that time he also began having some issues with his appetite and we later discovered that he had pancreatitis, which is a very painful ailment. His last year was pretty difficult, and the last three months in particular. He had to be hospitalized over Memorial Day weekend, and when he came home we had to medicate him and he never regained his appetite. We had to let him go on August 23rd, 2001, three weeks after he turned twelve years old. But little Brinkley had far more than his share of medical issues, beginning when we brought him home from the breeder.

As I stated in the first chapter of this book, when we went to pick Brinkley up from Lyle and Lois, his breeders, I noticed that he was itchy. I was not happy about this, but assumed that we were just dealing with an infestation of fleas, and since we had been through the mill with fleas with Murphy (due to the big open field behind our house on Coventry Drive, where we no longer lived when Brinkley joined our family), I just figured we would have to follow protocol to get rid of the fleas and then Brinkley would be fine. However, his first puppy visit to our new vet didn't reveal any fleas. We had Brinkley at home for about a month when the severity of the itching finally got so bad he couldn't sleep at night. The day before Thanksgiving, Brinkley's new vet ran some tests to find the source of his problem and discovered that it was sarcoptic mites. We were then able to get things turned around for him in short order, which was a great relief. But this was only the beginning of a lifetime of health issues for Brinkley.

In late summer the first year we had Brinkley, about a month before his first birthday, Brinkley hurt his back leg and began to limp. We took him to the vet and discovered that he had issues with his knees and received a referral to the veterinary clinic at the University of Illinois. We had to wait a month for an appointment, and after two weeks, Brinkley began getting around normally again. However, we went ahead and kept the appointment at the U of I just to have things checked out. I wish we had not! We had always had good care and kind doctors in the past when dealing with the U of I vet med clinic, so we had no reason to expect otherwise, but the doctor we saw that day was awful. To begin with, he had no bedside manner, and worst of all, he kept pulling on poor little Brinkley's legs, popping both knees in and out of the sockets to show us, and the students he was working with, that Brinkley had patellar luxation in both back legs. Tim and I were ready to come unglued by the time we left that appointment, with stern instructions to stop at the desk to schedule surgery for both knees. We were also informed that Brinkley would need a minimum of eight weeks recovery for each knee, with absolutely NO running or jumping during that time, or the surgery would be undone and additional surgery would be required. We could not see any way that we could successfully keep a one-year-old dog that quiet for that long, and since his knee had already returned to normal, could not justify putting him through all of that. We did NOT stop at the desk to schedule surgery, because in addition to this, neither Tim nor I wanted this particular surgeon anywhere near Brinkley ever again! We decided to see how things would go from there, and I am happy that we did because we were able to postpone this surgery until Brinkley was almost nine years old. And even then, we only had to have surgery on ONE knee.

Another issue that Brinkley had to deal with all of his life was lumps and bumps, and by that I mean growths and tumors. The first one he got was perhaps the most alarming, due to the size, and he got that one around the age of three. It was on the middle of his back, near the rump, and the vet discovered that it was a histiocytoma. He had to have surgery to remove it, and came home with a large shaved area and an incision about four inches long. Luckily, it was nothing to worry about; the stitches came out and his hair grew back in time, and all was well. While he was recovering, Tim and I borrowed an air mattress from my Mom and Dad and slept downstairs in the family room with Brinkley to ensure that he didn't try to bother his stitches. I don't think he could have gotten to them anyway since they were in the middle of his back, but it was a small sacrifice to make for our peace of mind, and Brinkley really enjoyed sleeping on the big air mattress with us! He thought that was the biggest doggy bed he had ever seen! Since we have a two-story house and have always been concerned about our boys running up and down the stairs (in addition to the fact that we knew Brinkley had bad knees), we had never allowed our dogs to sleep upstairs with us. But since both Murphy and Brinkley were crate-trained, they didn't mind having their own space in the downstairs bedroom just off the utility room, and both boys eventually ended up having the whole utility room area to roam and sleep in at night and when we were away at work. I wish the histiocytoma had been the first and only tumor that Brinkley had to endure, but he had all different shapes, sizes and types of tumors throughout his life. They would just come up out of nowhere and our vet would perform a fine needle aspirate to determine what they were, and then we would wait until they became large enough to be problematic and have them removed, sometimes more than one at a time. Fortunately, none of them were ever cancerous, although their names were always ominous, always with an "-oma" at the end.

In his later years, he developed a tumor above his eye, and also a smaller one under the same eye. The one on the top of his head kept getting larger and would bleed whenever he bumped it, and I would have to carefully clean away the dried blood when bathing him, and it finally became such an issue for him that we had both tumors removed. The poor little guy came home from the vet with an e-collar and a bunch of stitches on his head and under his eye, looking a lot like Frankenpuppy. We felt so sorry for him, but much relieved to be rid of the awful tumor. His final bout with the lumps and bumps was also in a terrible spot, this time right on his bottom. That time we had to be concerned about discomfort when he went potty, which was also not fun. We tried getting him to wear shorts; I even found a really cute pair with the Grinch and his little dog, Max, on them, since it was almost Christmas, but that met with limited success! So, we had to cover the family room carpet with sheets so that when he scooted we would not run the risk of getting blood on the carpeting. Our house would not have made the cover of any magazines that year, but it was more important to take good care of Brinkley. He had those stitches out just a few days before Christmas and was on the road to recovery, but as you will see later in this chapter that was not to last for long.

Among the issues that we doctored for at the U of I, at some point Brinkley had some trouble with his big, beautiful cocker spaniel eyes. Our vet had given us an ointment to use but also referred us to the specialists at the university. The eye doctor was a very pretty young lady, and all of her staff was also, and Brinkley simply stole all of their hearts! He was quite the ladies' man, and he was pretty crazy about them as well, almost to the point that it made his Mommy a little jealous, or I could have been if I had not liked them all so much! This was one of our most pleasant experiences at the U of I vet med clinic, as all of the staff was so engaging and seemed to love our boy as much as we did. Also, the outcome was favorable, so we were very grateful for all the help we received from them. But then, Brinkley's eyes, and those incredible, long lashes of his, always won a lot of hearts, including Sara at our vet's office who nicknamed him "Mr. Eyelashes"!

As previously stated, Brinkley began having problems with his knees even before his first birthday, but after that first episode, he didn't have any additional trouble until he was eight years old. It happened while I was working at Human Kinetics, and my job was on the ropes that spring. In late April, and at the point I was sure that I would not be keeping my job, Brinkley and I were on a walk when he injured his left back leg and began to limp again. Only this time it was different. Our vet found that the knee was in very bad shape and would need a double procedure. As previously diagnosed at the U of I, he had a luxating patella, but now, like Murphy, had also torn his cruciate ligament. Since we did not want to return to the orthopedic doctor at U of I, Dr. Revis consulted with Bill Smith, who had been Taffy's vet and also her teacher when she attended the university and Bill was head of surgery there. The decision was made that the two of them would perform the surgery on Brinkley's leg and the date was set for Friday May 7th so I would have the weekend to begin caring for Brinkley. As it turned out, again due to God's perfect timing, this was my last day at Human Kinetics, so I would be home to take care of my baby when he really needed me. We delivered him to Dr. Revis' office early that morning and I went to work to complete my final book and send it to the printer, and I left for the last time around 3:00 that afternoon. Later on we got the call that we could come pick Brinkley up, but it was recommended that he spend the night at the emergency clinic in town so they could monitor his pain meds and so forth that first night. We picked him up from the vet and dropped him off at the emergency clinic, and it was so hard to leave him there, but we knew it would be in his best interests to have professional care that first night. When they opened the next morning we were right there to pick up our baby and bring him home, and while I knew that I would feel overwhelmed, I now had the time off to take proper care of him. I was so grateful for this, and to top it all off, God also saw to it that we had the money to cover his surgery. The money I received as severance from HK was the exact amount we needed to cover Brinkley's vet bills…simply unbelievable, and as I see it, a miracle straight from the hand of God.

While I nursed Brinkley back to health following his knee surgery, I was back on the job hunt, doing my daily job search online, filling out my forms for the unemployment office so I could collect my weekly benefits, and had begun interviewing for jobs at Carle Hospital. I was looking for a position as a patient services representative, a fancy title meaning secretary, and had a total of seven interviews prior to being hired. My start date was set for August 2nd, 2010, which, incidentally, was Murphy's birthday! I was about to begin a new adventure! On a not-so-positive note, so was Brinkley, because later in August, he began to have issues with his skin, just when his knee seemed to be getting back to normal. It started out as three little dry-looking spots, which became kind of crusty. However, then it progressed and the spots began appearing in more and more areas and became problematic for Brinkley. We sought treatment at our vet's office and received another referral to a specialist in dermatology at the U of I, Dr. Santoro. Like the lady eye doctor, we fell in love with him; he was Italian and very charming, with a great sense of humor to lighten our concerns. Being a ladies' man, Brinkley didn't really pay any attention to Dr. Santoro when he first came in to talk with us, and it was a full fifteen minutes before he made eye contact with his new doctor. Dr. Santoro replied with "Suddenly, I'm in the room!" which still gives us a good laugh when we recount that first appointment! However, the skin condition was nothing to laugh about, as we began food trials to test for food allergies and weekly (and sometimes even more than weekly) bathing to treat for seborrhea. It was a grueling schedule for me, made even more so by the fact that I had to carry a forty-five pound dog up and down the stairs of our home to the bathtub. I was just blessed in the fact that Brinkley was such a compliant dog and never fought me when it came to any type of treatment for any of his ailments. This battle with the skin issue went on for the last two to two-and-a-half years of his life and we had just gotten pretty good control over it shortly before he left us. At one point in the course of treatment Dr. Santoro even had to show me how to administer injections. I thought I could do it, and Brinkley, with the patience of Job, even tolerated them for a while, but then we got a batch of bad needles, and when I stuck him, it made him cry. Well, that was more than I could take, and I decided we would not proceed with any more injections. He had simply been through too much.

As previously mentioned, in December of 2012, Brinkley had to undergo surgery for a tumor on his bottom, in a very delicate area. Dr. Revis did her usual, fine job with the procedure, and just before Christmas, he had his stitches out. We were finally able to uncover the family room carpeting, which had been covered with sheets to protect it from possible soilage during Brinkley's recovery, and enjoy the last couple days before Christmas with our house looking more like normal. We felt that Brinkley's recovery was our best present that year, and since his skin was also doing better, we had high hopes of things being better for him. It was not to be for long. He got through Easter, and my 50th birthday the day after, in fine shape and I was so grateful to still have him with us for this milestone. However, later in April, he began having problems with diarrhea, so we were back at the vet. She prescribed a medication for a couple weeks and things resolved, so once again we were hopeful. But then the symptoms returned with a vengeance in late May. I have recorded the ordeal of our last six weeks in the last regular chapter of this book, What Brinkley Taught Me About Saying Goodbye, so I will not rehash all the details here, but it was one of the most heart-wrenching times we have ever been through.

In all of Brinkley's trials with medical issues, which plagued him all of his life, he was never anything less than brave in the face of adversity, never complaining, never even crying out in pain, other than the one time I gave him the injection with a bad needle. I think, perhaps, that God knows which animals, just as He knows which people, will be able to bear up courageously in these kinds of situations, and selects them to teach the rest of us the grace of forbearance. I believe that is one of the reasons that everyone loved Brinkley the way they did. They could sense his infinite patience and the strength of his spirit. Brinkley had a profound effect on people, even people who were not dog-lovers. Our next door neighbor actually became emotional when she heard of Brinkley's passing. She had come to love how he would come to the fence whenever she was out in the yard and wait for her to speak to him, pat him or give him a treat through the little pass-through Tim created at the bottom of the fence. Another neighbor was a cat-lover, but simply adored Brinkley and would watch for him from her kitchen window and come out to visit whenever we would pass her house on a walk. This brave little dog stole all of our hearts, including most of the doctors who treated him for his various illnesses. He taught us all to be grateful in times of good health, and how to bear up graciously, and without complaint, in bouts with poor health. I will miss Brinkley forever until I meet him again at Rainbow Bridge, but it lightens my heart to know that he is now in a place of radiant good health, a condition that he so richly deserved, but never possessed, in his earthly life with us. I am anxiously awaiting the day we are reunited and can spend eternity together in Heaven, a place untarnished by sickness, complete with all the blessings of health and happiness forever.

Little Bits Of Joy – Family Time

I love my Mommy and Daddy, and there are a few activities that I enjoy doing with both of them, most especially sitting on the front porch together on nice days, or in the big chair-and-a-half in the family room on not-so-nice days. I have also been known to join Daddy in the hammock in the back yard in the summer time, or even better, when he decides to lounge in his really neat reclining lawn chair on the front porch, I am all over that! What makes this chair so special is that I can jump up on the foot of the chair before Daddy lays it back, and then when he does, it raises the foot up high so I can be tall and see everything that much better (unless, of course, we both fall asleep)! But my favorite activity with Daddy is a game we call "Hop on Pop", after the Dr. Seuss book. I wait until Daddy is stretched out on the floor, flat on his back, and come running up and hop on his chest! Sometimes I catch him by surprise and almost knock the wind out of him, and sometimes Mommy even participates in the game by clueing me in when Daddy is absorbed in a TV show and not watching out for me. She will silently get my attention, point at Daddy, and whisper the words, "Go get 'im!" and I will actually sneak in and pounce on him!

That always makes Mommy laugh, and after Daddy catches his breath, he laughs too!

As for Mommy, she loves that I am affectionate. I adore hugs, and I am a kissy dog, too. Grandma likes to tell Mommy, "Kiss that dog on the lips for me!" and Mommy is not afraid to do so! She's certainly not like Lucy in the Peanuts comic strips she loves so much, always shouting, "I've been kissed by a dog! I've got dog germs!" No, quite the contrary…as a matter of fact, when I was doctoring at the U of I veterinary medicine clinic (one of several times) for my skin issues, I had a wonderful Italian vet, Dr. Santoro, and Mommy was always tempted to get a t-shirt she saw in a catalog that said (in Italian, mind you), "I kiss my dog on the lips"! We even have a couple photos to prove it! Another favorite thing we do is have camp out nights on weekends. Mommy has a big duvet cover that Aunt Jean got for her, and we use it as a bed on the family room floor on Fridays and Saturdays and curl up together for the night. I get comfortable first, usually taking my spot right out of the middle like all dogs do, Mommy curls herself around me, and we are sound asleep in no time. In exchange for all of her love for me, all Mommy asks in return is that I not give my fuzzy little heart to anyone else. And because it is the ultimate goal of every good dog to bestow their heart, my Mommy and Daddy are the owners of mine.

What Brinkley Taught Me About...Just Being There

Just being there. It is one of the most valuable gifts we can offer one another, and so few of us humans know how to do it well. But our dogs...well, they are another story. While even the most well-meaning of our human friends can respond to our neediness with everything from a good-intentioned answer that doesn't really work for us to a remark that could hurt our feelings or even damage the relationship, the silent, understanding presence of our dogs consistently applies the balm of comfort to our jangled nerves and disquieted spirits. Not to underestimate or devalue our human friends, because it can be very helpful to have one with a good listening ear who will actually take the time to pay attention to what we are saying, take the various options into account, and offer up some good advice when we ask for it, or better yet, know how to ask the appropriate questions to help us find the best solution ourselves. Sometimes it is great to be able to bounce ideas off a fellow human being who knows us intimately enough for communication to be constructive, and who can respond in our own language to offer their thoughts. But there are plenty of times when the ideas of another are not feasible for us, or when words simply do not suffice or are not adequate for the unrest we feel within our souls. These are precisely the times when our dogs excel at knowing what to do. They have an uncanny ability to sense our moods, even when we think we are keeping our feelings under wraps and that no one else is picking up on them. It is then that our dogs will come and sit quietly beside us, or give us a look or a little nuzzle that lets us know that they are aware of what we are going through, and that they want to help. And my Brinkley was a master at sensing my emotions and in knowing just what to do. Brinkley and I went through so much together, sometimes when he would need my empathy, but many, many times when I needed his as well. And he would fix that deep brown gaze of his on me, reassuring me that he was there and that he would do whatever it took to see me through. And for this I owe him my eternal gratitude and my undying love.

I suppose I always knew that Brinkley was a good listener, and I always talked to him a lot, especially when we were alone in the house and I was cleaning or working on a project. I could never leave him alone for long, always taking breaks to pet him, or play with him, or just kiss his sweet little head. My dogs have always been the center of the universe for me, and the heart of our home, so I never can fathom how some people can own a dog and just resign them to a life outside in the yard, away from the rest of the family, or the "pack" that all dogs so long to be with. When we humans adopt a dog to live with us, we need to remember that we become their "pack", and that their main desire is to be with us. But I digress…back to Brinkley. Yes, I knew that he was a good listener, but he really proved how good when I lost my job. I was in a bad way, and every morning

I would get up and begin my day with prayer, sitting in the big chair-and-a-half with my little guy right beside me. I would put my arm around his furry shoulders for support, and we would take everything before the Lord in prayer...all of my fear over being without a job, the feelings of betrayal at what had happened to me, the burden of looking for another job...and Brinkley never faltered in his support for me. When we finished in prayer, I would get out my computer and begin my daily search for a new job, and I also had my job log to fill out each day for the unemployment office in order that I might keep my benefit check coming in. And Brinkley was right there for me throughout that process as well. He seemed to sense how difficult it was for me to try and reinvent myself in my mid-to-late forties, because several things had happened over the last few years I was at Hobbico that made it pretty much impossible for me to remain in graphic arts, the field I had trained in and worked in all my life. First of all, I had been in a supervisory position for the last several years I worked there, and when my role changed, I ceased doing the actual work on the computer and was instead responsible for proofing, routing and signing off the jobs, so I had not stayed current with the new computer programs for doing the work. Secondly, by the time I was laid off, the graphic arts field was not the booming career it had once been. Many companies were doing away with their art departments, choosing instead to employ an outside agency, or at the very least they were cutting back and streamlining their in-house departments to preserve their bottom line. So, after working in the same field for around 30 years total, I was trying to find a new place to fit, hopefully without having to return to school. No wonder I needed the steadfast support of my very, very good dog. And Brinkley never let me down. He was there for me all the way, listening when I needed to talk, or vent, or cry, and providing me with his sweet, calming presence when I just needed to be still and quiet my anxious thoughts.

Brinkley then proceeded to be there for me through several other job changes after I left Hobbico. After a short stint as a trainer at Curves in between full-time jobs, I thought I was going to be the happiest person ever in my new job as an assistant editor at Human Kinetics. But while things started off even better than I expected, they soon began to unravel. I eventually found myself bringing work home, not recording my time in order to get paid for it, just trying to keep up. And Brinkley would sit right there with me at the big coffee table in the family room, proofing those pages into the evening. But it was not enough, and I found out in April that I would not be keeping my job at HK. But immediately God's plan for the whole thing became apparent when at that exact time, Brinkley hurt his leg. And this time it was serious and would require surgery and an extensive recovery period. So, just as Brinkley had been there for me through all my job changes and woes, I would now be able to return the favor and be there for him, to care for him and love him back to health. And nothing could have been more important to me at that time. For one thing, I did not want anyone else in the family to have to assume such a big responsibility, or the trepidation that they might do something wrong that could cause further harm or more of a delay in Brinkley's recovery. This was a big deal and I felt it was essential that I fulfill it myself. And through my severance package with HK, God even provided the exact amount of money we would need for Brinkley's surgery. I would be able to be there for my little guy in more ways than one…to provide the finances he needed to get well, and the time and care he needed to be restored to health. And it just felt right to me to be able to be there for him, as he had so often been there for me.

When it comes to being there for someone, one of the most important elements we must exhibit is faithfulness, which is why our dogs excel in this area. I know that the Bible states that God created mankind in his image, but I also believe that there are characteristics of God that some of his other creations mirror in a way superior to ours, and faithfulness is one of those. After all, the Bible acknowledges that God is faithful to us even when we are unfaithful towards him, and isn't that just the type of faithfulness our dogs possess? How many stories have we all heard of dogs continuing to befriend owners who mistreat, or even harm them? Our dogs simply seem to find it much easier to forgive, even the most grievous offenses, than we do. It is just second nature to them. Now, of course, Brinkley never had to endure any such treatment in our home, where he was loved and cherished in a way that I believe all dogs should be, but he still proved faithful to us every day, and in every way. Because a faithful friend loves you at all times, whether you are up or down, having a good day or a bad one, even when you momentarily lose your temper and say something in anger that you really don't mean, or just need to have a good cry. Brinkley certainly experienced every nuance of our moods and feelings, and was a faithful friend in every instance. And like his Creator, God, Brinkley never wavered in his faithfulness to us, his human family, even when we were less than perfect and less than he deserved for us to be.

But back to that other key element of just being there; being a good listener, because Brinkley was among the best listeners ever, and not just in the hard times. Brinkley was a good listener in the everyday moments of life as well. He was my constant companion and my little shadow, whether I was off on a nature hike seeking out new vistas to photograph, sitting on the family room floor working on my latest poem, or enjoying a quiet moment with a cup of coffee on our front porch with Tim. And Brinkley had more than just a casual interest in what we were doing...he was all there, totally involved and fully in the moment with us. One of the activities he especially loved was when my parents would join us for a frozen mocha on the deck, and after Aunt Amy made the discovery that Brinkley liked licking the remaining whipped cream and chocolate off the straw when she finished her drink, all of us let him partake of our straws when we were finished, too! And I think it was as much of a treat for us, the enjoyment we got out of watching him savor that little bit of sweetness, as it was for him being on the receiving end! Because it was always a treat just being around Brinkley, and he was a more than a little bit of sweetness himself. And while it was obvious that he savored those chocolate-coated straws, it was also clear how much he savored just being there with all of us, and how he enjoyed our company. And unlike the human race, who are always a combination of good and not so good, in varying degrees, Brinkley was 100% sweetness. He just didn't seem to know any other way to be.

Another favorite activity for Brinkley, Tim and me was camping out. Now, mind you, I don't mean camping out as in pitching a tent and sleeping outdoors...I could never enjoy that, even as much as I love being outdoors, because I am complete and total mosquito bait! All I have to do is step outside, even for a moment, and they appear, as if out of thin air. Tim insists that he can sit on the porch indefinitely and they don't bother him in the least, but as soon as I come out I'm instantly slapping a mosquito. So, by camping out, I am referring to sleeping on the family room floor with Brinkley on the weekends. We would get out what we liked to call the "big doggy bed", which was a duvet cover my Aunt Jean bought for us, and spread it out on the floor, and Brinkley would pick his spot, usually right in the middle, where all dogs love to be. Then I would curl my body around his and fall asleep, and it was always the sweetest sleep ever because I could feel him near me. Ever since childhood I have been prone to having nightmares, but not when camping out with Brinkley. Perhaps the best guard dogs also have the ability to keep us safe from bad thoughts, even the subconscious kind. All I know is that we all loved camp out nights, and I have the most wonderful memories of them, especially at Christmas time when we would spread the big doggy bed under the Christmas tree and drift off to sleep under the twinkling lights. One favorite Christmas morning my best present was lazing with Brinkley under the tree, watching "Going My Way", one of my favorite old Bing Crosby movies. Among all the happy memories of special holiday moments with family and friends, this remembrance stands out as one of the simplest, yet most profoundly joyful, times of all.

Speaking of joy, Brinkley just brought all of the joy he took from life with him everywhere he went. I have heard some people described as "old souls" as a term of endearment, and if I understand the use of the term properly, I think it also describes certain very special dogs such as Brinkley. I think he started out life as an old soul, even as a puppy possessing a type of wisdom and understanding that usually only comes with age and the seasoned character that brings, but that only a handful, even of humans, ever acquire. You could tell just by looking into his eyes, because those eyes looked directly into his soul, which was deep and profound, and brimming with compassion and understanding. I am convinced that anyone who doesn't believe that our dogs possess a soul has either never owned or truly connected with a dog, because it is impossible to deny if this has ever been your privilege. Because our dogs, if given even just a chance, will prove their loyalty beyond the shadow of a doubt, and often even to the most undeserving people. Because, unlike people, dogs don't hold a grudge, they don't harbor ill feelings, and they don't get fed up and move on if we disappoint them, even repeatedly. Because it is a dog's ultimate goal to please us, to make our lives happier, and to bestow their hearts, and if we are truly blessed, we may be the grateful recipients of this best of all gifts.

Little Bits Of Joy – I Never Met A Stranger

Mommy has always loved taking me for walkies, and I love them too…as a matter of fact, I love them so much that I have always been quite a "puller", always eager for the next scent along the way! The other thing that both of us love is meeting new people on our walks. I am a people dog and have never met a stranger that I couldn't charm…at least not when I could get them to notice me and come over to give me a pet. There are, of course, the few distracted folks that you sometimes encounter, who are too busy listening to something on their earbuds, or too zoned out in some other galaxy to notice a cute cocker spaniel trying to get their attention…on occasion, when we cross paths with someone like that, I keep up the full-court press to catch their eye, then sit down in bewilderment as they pass by, unaware of the opportunity they just missed! I simply cannot grasp when Mommy tells me that "not EVERYONE wants to pet me"…what could be wrong with these people? However, most of the time I am like the dog in the movie "Because of Winn-Dixie", who makes friends for his little human companion India Opal wherever they go. It was because of me that Mommy became friends with our neighbor down at the corner of Phinney and Branch, Becky and her husband, Jim…Becky is a cat person, but couldn't resist coming out to the street to meet me one day when she noticed me pulling Mommy up her driveway to say hello! Well, they became the best of friends after that, and I always look forward to seeing her whenever we get near her house. And the feeling is mutual for Becky, as she watches for me to round the corner onto Branch from her kitchen window! Mommy and I have spent many happy hours visiting with Becky and Jim, and they have become beloved friends of Mommy and Daddy, all because of me. And as every good dog knows, every human can use all the friends he or she can get, and I definitely recognize my ability to assist my family in that respect!

What Brinkley Taught Me
About...How To Treat Others

Most of us remember from childhood our mothers teaching us to treat others the way we would like to be treated ourselves, and sometimes when we encounter difficult people, doing this can prove to be a challenge. And it seems to me that, along with our mothers, that our dogs have a lot to teach us about this subject. Just like people, dogs are born with different personalities, and some just seem to have more patience with other people and/or dogs. Brinkley was such a dog. He came to us already friendly and engaging, having been raised by an elderly couple with grandkids who took him outside to play and interacted with him. And he had come to know my husband and me before coming home with us, since Tim found him right after his birth and went to visit him for the first time when he was only ten days old and didn't even have his eyes open yet! Together we made two more visits, at four weeks and six weeks, prior to bringing him home at eight weeks. And unlike our first cocker spaniel together, Murphy, we made a conscious decision to socialize Brinkley immediately. When we got Murphy, there was a big parvo scare going on, and we were advised not to expose Murphy, even to other people, until his immune system was fully in place. We now know that the best time to socialize a puppy is in the first two to four months, so Murphy missed this window entirely. Since we didn't want our new puppy to be fearful of, or aggressive toward, people he did not know, we decided to have as many of our friends as possible stop by the house when Brinkley first came home, and what a difference it made!

Of course, Brinkley's first interaction with other people was with members of our immediate family the day he came home. We got up early and made the drive to Bloomington-Normal and were home with our new baby while the day was still young. Since we were living next door to my parents on Brookshire by this time, they came over right away to meet their new little grandson. My Aunt Jean, who lived nearby at Colony West, also stopped by that first day to meet her new little nephew. The whole family thought he was pretty special. And everyone who met Brinkley from that day on seemed to have the same opinion! When the new work week began, we took Brinkley in for his first vet visit to make sure he was in good health, and as he was to do for the rest of his life, he charmed everyone there as well! We started Brinkley off with a new vet, who was recommended to us by Tracei at the emergency clinic where Murphy had been treated for the last few months we had him. Tracei had been an answer to our prayers when Murphy was turned away at his regular vet's office when he became seriously ill just before Memorial Day weekend. It was suggested that we take him to the emergency clinic, and we couldn't have been happier with the care he received there. While Murphy's regular vet had developed an attitude of mistrust in him following the bite incident of our former neighbor, in which he really was not to blame, Tracei immediately got down on the floor with him, got right in his face, and loved on him. Murphy, Tim and I all fell in love with her at our first meeting. Because after all, dogs know which people like them, and they recognize the difference when people trust them and when they don't. Tracei was obviously in tune with animals, and she knew that Murphy was a good boy who just needed a little love to accompany his medical treatment. Therefore, we assumed that she was also a good judge of character when it came to people, and we were correct. When we made the decision to get a new puppy, we asked Tracei for recommendations on a new vet clinic, and she gave us the names of two people at the same office. We started out with Dr. Wolfe, who saw Brinkley for his very first visit. When we arrived for our appointment, Brinkley started out by charming the girls who checked us in at the front desk, and proceeded to have the same effect on the doctor and everyone else he met that day. I suppose part of this reaction was due to the fact that few things in life are cuter than a five pound cocker spaniel puppy, but we were off to a great start, and what an achievement to have a puppy who actually didn't mind going to the vet!

Also among Brinkley's first acquaintances were my friends from Hobbico, where I worked at the time. My boss and friend of many years, Julie, stopped by to meet him while he was still very small, in part because, like many people who love dogs, she was enchanted by "puppy breath"! Those of you, and I assume this would be the entire readership of this book since it is about a dog, who have ever raised a puppy, or ever even been around one, know just what I mean! It defies description…it just simply has to be experienced. And it doesn't last, which is why they call it "puppy breath", not "doggy breath", which has a far lesser perceived appeal! Well, Julie was tickled with Brinkley, as was everyone he met! Another early visitor was Trudy, a member of my inner circle at Hobbico, and although Trudy can't have a dog herself because of her allergies, she has always loved my boys and has been able to spend time with them as they do not shed and therefore do not aggravate her condition as long as she is diligent to wash her hands after petting them. Trudy had been Murphy's Aunt as well, and had mourned his loss with me, so she was thrilled to meet her new little nephew! Julia, a co-worker from Russia, also stopped by with her daughter Lucy, who was then also fairly young. I will never forget Lucy questioning me about why little Brinkley wanted to bite at her fingers when she tried to pet him, and I told her, "Because he's a puppy"! He was simply at that puppy teething age where they try to taste absolutely everything they come into contact with! So, while Lucy was a little apprehensive at that first meeting, she and Brinkley went on to become the very best of friends. I have lots of great pictures of the two of them over the course of time as Lucy would join us for parties, everything from funny shots of Lucy holding her fingers over Brinkley's head to simulate bunny ears to sweet photos of Lucy with her arm around Brinkley's shoulders, holding him close. And because Lucy and Brinkley grew up together, I believe that Lucy became one of Brinkley's greatest loves, and that he actually pined for her when she got older and didn't come to all of the get-togethers that we girls had. I will never forget their last visit, when she stopped by the house during a party. Brinkley hadn't seen her in some time, and he just about lost his mind with joy seeing her again. And to think it was the last time. I am so grateful for the precious memories I have of the two of them interacting over the years whenever she would get together with us. She is a darling girl, and my darling boy loved her so much.

Speaking of the girls at Hobbico, they were over often for parties in those days, so they were all close friends of Brinkley's, and he liked each of them for unique and different reasons. In addition to Aunt Trudy and Aunt Julia, there was Aunt Dawn, Aunt Vicky, and Aunt Amy. Aunt Dawn is herself a huge fan of dogs, and has a little Bichon Frise named Molly whom she also considers to be and treats as a child. Aunt Dawn would even extend invitations for other members of the group to bring their dogs to play with Molly when she hosted parties, and while I never took Brinkley with me, it was nice to know that he was welcome. Aunt Dawn always doted on Brinkley when she came to our house and lavished him with attention, and of course he loved that. She was a great playmate for Brinkley when he was little and wasn't afraid to rough-house with him…she recognized the advantages of wearing a puppy out a bit so he could burn off that excess energy and then crash and burn as puppies are prone to do! Aunt Vicky was Brinkley's aunt of choice when he wanted to sit and be still and enjoy a nice, long petting session. Aunt Vicky has a calm, quiet personality and Brinkley would often retreat to her side when we girls were in the thick of visiting, and he knew that Aunt Vicky would just let him be, even when the conversation would become more animated and we were laughing louder than he might like. He could count on Aunt Vicky to be his rock in the midst of the craziness! Aunt Amy is also a dog-lover, and had two pugs, Tucker and Oliver, who were the center of the universe at her house! After a while of the dogs being her only children, she and her husband, Mike, had a little human daughter join their family. Her name is Lily, and from the time she was born she often joined us at parties, so she and Brinkley also became fast friends. It was wonderful, especially when Lily was small and right at eye level with Brinkley, to have such a gentle dog, and one whom we knew didn't have any issues with his temperament. We never had to fear that Brinkley would turn on Lily. He was a total sweetheart and had endless patience with children as well as adults. As Lily got older, she took note of the fact that Brinkley liked to lay down on the cool, smooth surface of our big, burled oak coffee table in the family room, and one Christmas I took some really cute pictures of the two of them sitting up there together…too funny!

We also have lots of great pictures of Brinkley and the girls from Hobbico from the numerous parties we had back then. Brinkley was quite a ham when he was younger and would always want to join in the fun when we were taking pictures, so he was always a featured guest in those photos! Some of the most memorable were a series where Aunt Trudy was trying to hug him to keep him with her in the photo and he was squirming to get free, a number of photos from various parties of him sitting next to Aunt Vicky enjoying his pets, a really pretty picture of him with Aunt Julia leaning in for a close up, photos of him interacting with Aunt Dawn, and still others of him sitting with Aunt Amy and Lily. There are two series of photos we took on the porch swing in our back yard, one of which I shot, and for the other we recruited my husband, Tim, to do the photography so all of us girls could be in the pictures. In the series I shot, Dawn and Julia were sitting on the swing with Brinkley in between them. Well, then the girls in the back row decided it would be funny to make bunny ears with their fingers above the heads of the girls on the swing. When Dawn and Julia discovered what they were doing back there, Dawn decided to hold Brinkley's great big cocker spaniel ears up over his head, and things just progressed from there! Bunny ears also got started in the second series of pictures on the porch swing, the photos that Tim helped shoot. I don't know what it was about posing on the swing that caused this behavior, but it seemed to happen each time we did it! In this series, I am kneeling next to Brinkley on the ground in front of the swing, and the girls in the back row are acting up again, holding their fingers above the heads of the girls on the swing. In one of the pictures, Brinkley looks like he is pleading for someone to rescue him from this crazy situation he has found himself in! Brinkley was always a very expressive dog, and you can just tell from his face in that picture that he thinks that we have all lost our minds! But, patient little saint that he was, he always bore up under whatever circumstances he found himself in, whether they were just silly like this one, or serious like his various health conditions. He just simply dealt with everything gracefully, and taught me so much about how to do the same.

Lucy and Lily weren't the only children that Brinkley made friends with…there were also Maggie and Josh across the street. When Jeff and Katie moved in, Maggie was really little and Josh had not come along yet, but over the course of time, they became regular visitors to see Brinkley when they spotted us on the front porch. Brinkley was always happy to see them, and they loved giving him treats and throwing his ball for him to fetch, and there was never any concern that he would be anything but gentle with them when taking treats from their hands or surrendering the ball for them to toss. And just like with Lily when she was small and right at eye level with Brinkley, we had absolute trust in Brinkley's temperament and knew that he would be sweet with Maggie and Josh. I really think it was a big plus that Brinkley was raised around Lois and Lyle's grandkids and that they helped care for him from the time he was born. Apparently he had learned to love children early in his life and this was one of the best characteristics of his personality.

However, Brinkley did not limit himself to sharing his love with children. He also had a profound impact on the elderly folks he came into contact with. We made more than a couple wonderful friends, and lasting relationships, with older people we met while on walks in the neighborhood. Our best friendship evolved with a couple who lived on the corner of Phinney and Branch, Jim and Becky. They had a large lot and enjoyed landscaping it, so they were outdoors a lot. And while they were cat people, having a beautiful, Maine coon cat named Fringes, Brinkley would not allow them to ignore that he was an immensely friendly dog and that he was intent on making them fall in love with him! He wouldn't settle for just a hello in passing, but insisted that we go up the driveway to meet them and carry on a bit of conversation! And he made good on his intentions, because both of them came to find him irresistible, and soon we had a great friendship established because of Brinkley's determination to bring us together with people whom we otherwise likely would have never met. Becky even took to looking for Brinkley whenever she was working at her kitchen window, and would make a special trip outdoors to see him and talk awhile whenever we were out for a walk. And even if she was not already outside, Brinkley would drag me up their driveway in the hope that someone would see him and come out! I believe that our friendship came to mean even more to Becky after Jim was diagnosed with cancer and later passed away, since she was now on her own and looked forward to Brinkley's visits all the more. Unfortunately, Becky did not last long living by herself in that big house with all the yard work, and not long after Jim's passing she also became rather frail, struggling with issues with her balance and sustaining several fairly serious falls. She soon had to sell the house and move to assisted living, so it was never quite the same walking by her house after that. And Brinkley never got over looking for his old friends. He would still try to pull me up the driveway for the rest of his life, even though Jim and Becky were no longer there.

Another elderly friend we met while on our walks was Sue. She lived just a little further down Branch Drive from Jim and Becky, and was also outdoors on occasion, although never as often as they were. Sue was a tiny, sweet lady and was immediately enamored with Brinkley. We had several very nice interactions with Sue, and Brinkley would always check to see if she happened to be out when we walked past her house. I truly believe that Brinkley would have been a perfect therapy dog, since he was so sweet and gentle with everyone he met. I wish I would have pursued finding out what kind of training he would have needed in order to go into the local nursing homes for visits with the residents, because he would have been the ideal candidate for this type of work. And I can only imagine how many lives he would have enriched by doing so, and how many lonely people would have eagerly looked forward to a visit with my sweet, selfless little guy.

And Brinkley didn't limit his friendships to people he met on walks; he also made friends close to home. Our next door neighbor to the south, Nedra, also became fast friends with Brinkley. We wanted to start off on the right foot with Nedra when we first got Brinkley, because Murphy was already six years old when we moved to Brookshire and since he did not know Nedra, he would bark at her when she was out working in her back yard, and we knew she probably did not appreciate that. So, when we brought Brinkley home, we made a point to introduce him to Nedra right away so he would be used to seeing her next door. We also gave Nedra treats and little baggies of his chow so she could feed him, and this became such fun for the two of them that Tim cut a little space out of the bottom of the fence and installed a "treat tray" for Nedra to place the food on so Brinkley could eat it! We would also stop and visit with Nedra whenever she was out working in her front yard when we were out for a walk, and that was often since she also takes meticulous care of her lawn. I knew that Nedra had really come to like Brinkley, and interacting with him, but I had no idea how much until I had to inform her of his passing. She said that she had a feeling something must be amiss because she had noticed our outdoor lights were on a lot more frequently and in the middle of the night those last couple weeks when he had to make frequent outings to go potty, and she became emotional at the news that he was gone. And it really shouldn't have surprised me, since Brinkley had this very profound effect on everyone he became friends with over the course of his almost twelve year life, but it did touch me deeply how much Nedra had come to love our boy.

Brinkley was even gracious at the vet's office, something that even the most easy-going among dogs can have issues with. As previously stated, Brinkley started off well at his very first visit to Country View Veterinary Clinic, two days after we brought him home, by charming the girls at the front desk, Leesa and Amanda. Amanda soon went on to become Brinkley's girlfriend there, as she was the vet tech most frequently involved in his care when he would visit. Dr. Wolfe, his first veterinarian, soon became our hero when she was able to track down the cause of his itching, which became intense in November of the year we brought him home, when he was about three months old. She was extremely thorough in her testing to determine the problem, which turned out to be sarcoptic mites, visible only through a microscope. About the time Brinkley was due to be neutered, Dr. Wolfe and her husband, a veterinary cardiologist at the University of Illinois who had participated in Murphy's care during the last couple months of his life, moved to California to be closer to family, so Dr. Revis took over Brinkley's care, and we couldn't have been happier with either of them. Tracei at the Animal Emergency Clinic had been right on target with both recommendations. We continued care at Country View until Dr. Revis left, and at first we could not find out where she had gone, but finally we were able to locate Leesa, who had also left, and discovered that Dr. Revis had started her own practice in Mahomet.

By that time we had had a couple visits with other doctors at Country View but weren't happy with a recent diagnosis and recommendation that we put Brinkley on a daily dose of Benadryl, since we didn't want him spending the rest of his life groggy from medication. So in spite of the longer drive, we followed Dr. Revis, and I believe we were very wise in doing so. After all, Dr. Revis had taken care of Brinkley from the time he was six months old, and Brinkley had always had a myriad of health issues, so she was certainly the most familiar with his history and the best suited to continue caring for him. And Brinkley just continued to charm the girls he met at the new office…he even made a new girlfriend there, Sara, who subsequently nicknamed him "Mr. Eyelashes"!

Brinkley also had an entourage of different groomers… not by choice, but by necessity, as we had to keep switching as his current groomer would move on and we would be forced to find another. He started off with Johnsy, a very nice lady who was the groomer at Country View vet when we first started taking Brinkley there as a puppy. She did his first groom, sending him home with a snazzy little bow on his collar, and we continued with her until she left. Unfortunately, our next choice was not a good one, but we didn't know that right away. This groomer's shop was located right next to the railroad tracks in Savoy, and she also boarded dogs, so the atmosphere was quite noisy, with the trains going by so close to the shop and the incessant barking of the boarded dogs. I used to drop Brinkley off in the morning and pick him up at lunch time so he wouldn't have to spend the whole day there, but one day when I arrived to get him, he hadn't even been touched. Instead, the lady who owned the shop was having a meltdown, crying and practically in hysterics because she was short-staffed and as she stated, just unable to handle all the grooming appointments. And while I felt sorry for her, I just wished she had told me before I dropped Brinkley off and he sat there in a cage for hours awaiting a groom that never happened. In desperation since his hair was already overgrown and it was the middle of summer, I located a groomer at a pet shop in a local strip mall, and she did a good enough job and we liked her, but she didn't stay either. We continued going there to a different groomer who also didn't stay, and then finally began driving Brinkley to Monticello to see Lois, who came to us by recommendation of Aunt Dawn, since Lois was Molly's groomer. We fell in love with Lois, and she with Brinkley, and she took excellent care of him for several years, until at some point when we made the drive and found that Lois was not there. She had posted a sign on her door stating that she was out due a medical emergency, and we later discovered that she had broken her leg, but since it was summer again, we couldn't let Brinkley's hair continue to grow until we could get another appointment with Lois. As we returned to town after the drive back from Monticello, I spotted the sign for Bark Avenue, a grooming shop attached to a lovely home bordering Duncan Road. On a whim I said to my Dad, "Let's stop here and I'll run in and see if we can get Brinkley an appointment". Jan, the owner of the shop, said that she usually only groomed smaller dogs, with her specialty being shih-tzus, but when she met Brinkley, she instantly fell in love with him and agreed to book an appointment with the new assistant she had just hired. Brinkley had a couple appointments with her until she left to begin working with a mobile groomer, but by then Jan was so fond of Brinkley that she agreed to groom him herself. This turned out to be very convenient as her shop was very close to home for us, and was especially so during Brinkley's last three years when he was diagnosed with skin allergies and had to be bathed and groomed much more frequently. I bathed him at home as often as multiple times per week and Jan kept his hair short to make it easier to care for his skin condition. It was during the years when Jan groomed Brinkley that we discovered that he was also good around other dogs, even though he had not previously been in this situation. At Jan's shop, the dogs were not caged but were allowed to roam freely behind the counter with the other dogs there for grooming that day, and Brinkley even took to that with ease. One of the most charming stories that Jan shared with us was one day when she had, as she described him, a "little shy guy" by the name of Chester there on the same day as Brinkley, and Brinkley allowed Chester to walk around with him. I was so proud of my boy when I heard that! When we lost Brinkley just days after his last groom with Jan in July of 2013, on a day we all felt as though he had made a turn for the better, I think it was almost as hard on Jan as it was on us, such had been his effect on her.

In all of his interactions throughout his life, Brinkley had always shown his inimitable charm and grace, even in the tough times. I will never forget the report I received from my Mom after she and Dad had the difficult task of taking Brinkley for his ultrasound testing at the University of Illinois, just shortly before we decided that he had been through enough and that we would not pursue further testing. He had just gotten his appetite back after weeks of struggling with it and then had to be denied food prior to testing, which was supposed to be that morning but was then postponed until mid-afternoon. My Mom was beside herself at that point and told the doctor so, but she told me, through her tears, that as she stood there watching the tech lead Brinkley away down the hall for testing that he marched off just like the brave little soldier that he was, even after all he had been through. And so it is that I can declare that my courageous little dog taught me more about strength, even in the tough times, than most people I have known. And that also goes for being a great role model in regards to how to treat others, whether of the human or canine variety, in a myriad of different circumstances.

Little Bits Of Joy -- Call Me Mr. Eyelashes

My eyelashes have always garnered lots of attention, but just recently Sara at my vet's office began calling me Mr. Eyelashes. Sara and I deepened our relationship over the last month when I visited her every day except for one the first week of June. I got very sick with some kind of icky stomach bug and decided I didn't want to eat for a week. I also lost interest in my water bowl and kept becoming dehydrated, so Mommy, Daddy, and my grandparents shuttled me back and forth to the vet's office for sub-Q fluids. For those readers without a medical degree, those are subcutaneous fluids. One nice thing about them is that you don't have to have your front leg shaved for an IV, and the best thing about them is that you don't have to stay at the vet's office while your family goes home without you! Anyway, my Grandma is the reason that I have these tremendous, long lashes, because she's been known to threaten my groomer (although not to her face!) if I make a wrong move and she accidentally shaves one off and then has to rectify the situation by trimming the other side off to even me up! Lucky for Janice (my groomer), this has only happened a time or two, and Grandma was revealed to be all bark and no bite since she didn't really go after Janice in retaliation! Not that she ever would have, since Janice is the most wonderful, caring groomer a dog could ever hope for, and has taken exquisite care of me for years. My entire family loves Janice, and we are all very grateful to her for keeping me comfortable with a haircut every five weeks. At any rate, I have charmed many ladies with my eyelashes over the years, including a team of veterinary medical students and the lead doctor (all young ladies) in the eye department at the University of Illinois, where I was once seen for some issues with my big brown peepers. Actually, it seems that wherever I go, I am noticed for my lashes. So I have Grandma to thank for them, and because I like the attention, I am appreciative of that! And thanks to Sara for the additional nickname, because, as every good dog knows, any attribute we have that creates a bond between our humans and others of their kind is a good attribute indeed!

What Brinkley Taught Me About...Saying Goodbye

The last week of May, Wednesday the 29th to be exact, Brinkley had a recurrence of diarrhea. He had suffered a bout with diarrhea at the end of April which had quickly, and seemingly completely, resolved with a two-week round of metronidazole, an antibiotic prescribed by our vet, Dr. Revis. The day it recurred, he had an appointment with his groomer, Janice, so I informed her about it in a note I always send to alert her of any issues he is currently having. He continued having problems for the rest of the week, and by Saturday and Sunday, I was taking him outside every two hours, including nights. Late Sunday afternoon, I remembered that I had given him Imodium back in April to relieve the symptoms, so I began trying that, but it was clear that nothing was helping. On Monday, June 3rd, I called in to work so Tim and I could take him to the vet. Once there, we discovered that he was dehydrated, so they administered subcutaneous fluids and sent us home, but we had to return again the next day after fasting him overnight so Dr. Revis could do a blood panel. On Tuesday morning he was already dehydrated again, so he had another round of subcutaneous fluids. We managed to stay out of the vet's office on Wednesday, only to return again on Thursday for more fluids. Brinkley's water intake simply could not keep up with the frequency of his diarrhea, and nothing that had worked in April was having any effect this time. Things were so bad on Friday, June 7th, that my Mom and Dad had to take Brinkley to Dr. Revis again, this time leaving him all day to receive IV fluids. The report at noon was dismal. It sounded as though Brinkley had pancreatitis, the disease that had taken Murphy from us, along with the possibility of issues with the liver and small and large intestine. Mom called me at work in great distress to pass along the news, and I went into a patient room at the clinic where I worked at the time to return the call to Dr. Revis. Mom also called Tim at work to let him know the findings. He was off at 3:00 that day, so I asked if I could leave early as well so that we could go and pick Brinkley up. When we arrived, Dr. Revis didn't seem as grim as we expected with the possible diagnosis being what it was. She understood the baggage that we came into the situation with, based upon what had happened to Murphy, but she really felt that Brinkley could be supported until he could get back on his feet. She recommended that we take Brinkley to the University Of Illinois Small Animal Hospital to stay the weekend and continue receiving IV fluids. She said that once he was feeling better there were options we could pursue in terms of diet that would help him. So, instead of losing him that night as we expected we might on the way to Dr. Revis' office, we transported him to the U of I, where he underwent another examination and more tests. On their advice, we left him there and went for a late dinner, awaiting their call as to what treatment they would recommend.

When we received their call, the doctor there felt that he was well enough to go home for the weekend, and that we could call at any time if he became dehydrated again or his symptoms began to worsen. And while I was grateful to be able to take him home, I also felt the burden of being responsible for knowing if he needed to go back in over the weekend. The next morning I was up early cooking chicken and rice, which was the recommended diet to encourage him to begin eating again. He had hardly touched a bite of anything for the last week and was quite weakened from the whole experience. We did have some success with that, so we thought, or more accurately, hoped, that we were gaining ground, although the very next week we faced the next obstacle in finding out what was making him sick. On Monday, June 10th, Brinkley had to undergo an ultrasound at the U of I. We weren't sure about the date and time it would be scheduled over the weekend since they do not schedule such appointments on weekends, so we had to wait and have my Mom call on Monday morning. She was told to bring him in at 11:00 AM, but then the test was not done until much later that afternoon, so Brinkley, who had just begun to have an appetite again after a whole week of not eating, had to be fasted overnight and until after his test was conducted. We were all pretty upset about that anyway, and then about the diagnosis, which was totally inconclusive and came with a recommendation that we could proceed with a colonoscopy, which would be both invasive and expensive, including a hospital stay of three to five days. We knew that Brinkley was far too weak to survive an exhaustive test like that, and none of us were willing to put him through that, especially since they could not guarantee that they would discover the cause of his illness, or be able to cure it if they did. And so Brinkley ate chicken and rice for the next couple weeks as he began another, longer round of metronidazole, this time to be for six weeks total. He was also given a prescription medication especially for dogs to control his diarrhea, and that seemed to help. For a couple weeks he showed a gradual improvement, and we began to feel a bit of relief. But it was not to last.

On Monday, June 24th, just when Brinkley's stools had almost returned to normal, we had the thunderstorm to end all thunderstorms. It began at 4:00 PM and I had to work late that evening, so when I left the clinic at 6:00 I didn't know if I would be blown away, drowned by the horizontal sheets of rain, or struck by lightning on the way to my car. I am not afraid of storms, but this was one of only two storms that actually struck terror in my heart. And Brinkley had a terrible fear of storms that had begun when he went to a grooming shop that was right on the train tracks. We never figured out if it was train noise that started his anxiety or possibly the barking of the boarded dogs there, but he was never the same after that experience. When I arrived at home, my Dad was with him, but it was of little comfort to Brinkley. He had barely eaten anything at lunch and refused any dinner or snack later that night as the storm raged on until after 1:00 AM. Tim had the late shift that day and sat up with Brinkley when he got home after midnight so I could get some rest for the next day at work, and he said it was 4:00 AM before Brinkley was able to settle down and go to sleep. It was all downhill again from there, and his diarrhea and lack of appetite returned. We were back where we had started.

Brinkley did seem to rally a bit again around the 4th of July. We decided to try the canned food that we had given him to supplement his dry food when he was a year old because he had always had a sensitive stomach. To our delight, he loved it, but it didn't last. We did have a wonderful first week of July with him, sitting on the edge of our pool that weekend with Brinkley lying next to us, listening to the classic rock station, which had just come back on the air years after I had grown up listening to it, and talking for several hours. It was an unseasonably cool day, kind of cloudy, but really comfortable for Brinkley and for us to spend some quality time outside, where we all loved best to be. I treasure that weekend, because it was to be the last of our good times together.

Just when we thought that Brinkley liked the canned food enough to make it his steady diet, and I had purchased a case of it, he lost interest in eating again. The following week, on Thursday night, he refused to eat at all, even when I made chicken and rice. He was just about at the end of his six week course of metronidazole, still on his diarrhea medication, and now, once again, not doing any better.

I think I mourned the loss of Brinkley periodically for all of those six weeks, because I just didn't see any real progress. He would rally and then fall back. One night in particular stands out in my mind. We were outside on one of his many potty breaks, and I noticed that there were a few fireflies blinking out in the yard. The poor little guy was walking around in the squat position he had become so accustomed to, and those little lightning bugs made me cry because I remembered how he used to dance and twirl around as a puppy trying to catch them. It seemed like only yesterday. How did we get from there to here so quickly? And then in the distance I heard the train whistle, which we always refer to as Murphy's train. That goes back to the days he spent in the Animal Emergency Clinic when he was so sick over Memorial Day weekend. When Tim would go over to visit him and take him for short walks outside, Murphy would bark at that train. And so, that night, in those circumstances, I felt like Murphy was calling Brinkley to come and join him, and I just was not ready to let him go yet. But I knew it was coming.

On Friday, July 12th, everything went south. Brinkley was back to not eating at all, and even the batch of chicken and rice I made that evening could not tempt him. He also became very restless and unable to sleep. We went outside every hour that night. I was beside myself that next morning and not sure what to do since it was the weekend and Dr. Revis was not in the office, but my Mom took the initiative and called the clinic. The girls were able to reach Dr. Revis at home and she called me to discuss what was going on. Dr. Revis is the most wonderful, understanding person, and she took the time that Saturday morning to help me develop a plan to get Brinkley through the weekend. I still had three half-tablets of an appetite enhancer that Dr. Revis had administered on June 7th when he was in her office for the day for IV fluids, and she told me I could use one every twenty-four hours, which would get us through Saturday, Sunday and Monday. She told me that if he was feeling nauseous, the medication would help with that. She also recommended a Pepcid twice daily for stomach acid. He would continue the metronidazole through the end of its course the next Tuesday, and the lomotil for diarrhea. Tim had the late shift that day at work, and was home with us until 1:30, so I filled him in on the plan. Around 11:00, I gave Brinkley the appetite booster and a Pepcid, and then at noon, I offered some chicken and rice. He ate a saucerful, and a little more I added after that. I was feeling pretty positive. The idea was to get us through until Monday when Dr. Revis was going to call the doctor at the U of I who had conducted the ultrasound to get her perceptions on the liver aspirate. Tim went off to work and I continued with my usual Saturday activities of cleaning house. My Mom called me with the idea to take Brinkley for a joy ride in the Eddie (their Ford Explorer Eddie Bauer edition SUV, which Brinkley loved to ride in). She and Dad had done that a few times recently, driving through neighborhoods with pretty, new homes, and it seemed to really cheer Brinkley up. Around 5:00, I thought Brinkley was restless again and that a ride would help his boredom, so Mom and Dad came over and picked us up. Brinkley sat up and looked out the window for a while, but then laid down on the seat next to me, losing his interest. He was obviously still not feeling well, but I didn't mention anything to Mom and Dad. When we returned home, we discussed me coming over to have dinner and then Mom and I would take a walk, but then changed plans and decided to walk first since it was early for dinner for us, only about 6:00. Dad agreed, as he always did, to sit with Brinkley on the front porch while we took our walk.

When Mom and I returned in about an hour, my typically cool-as-a-cucumber-about-everything Dad was visibly agitated. He described that Brinkley had been unable to rest, pacing up and down the porch, and that he had been shaking. He had done the same for a while in the morning, but I assumed that he just got chilled since the temperatures were below normal for July that day. But it hardly seemed right this late in the afternoon and since the sun had come out and warmed things up. Brinkley went to the door and scratched to get in, so Dad took him out to the back yard for another potty break. When he returned, he was very upset. He said, "You better put this poor guy down tonight". I was stunned. My plan was falling apart. I was not prepared to lose Brinkley on Saturday night. I was hoping to keep him going through the weekend until the doctors could talk on Monday, and now I was facing the most horrible decision of my life a couple days too soon. I was especially worried about calling Tim to have him leave work and meet us, because I knew he was not going to understand this change in plans either. But the more I thought about it, I could not bear the risk that Brinkley might go into a seizure, or begin crying out in pain, during the night. Friday night had been bad enough, and Saturday looked to be even worse. I also did not want to call Dr. Revis in the middle of the night. She had been kind enough to tell me I could call her cell phone if things went to pieces, so I went inside to get her number and make the awful call.

When I returned to the porch, I was unable to speak without crying, so Mom spoke with Dr. Revis. We made a plan to meet her at the clinic at 8:00, and then I called Tim. He was on dinner break, but returned my call as we were leaving with Brinkley, and agreed to meet us there. Brinkley laid quietly on the back seat of the Eddie with me for that last trip, never making a peep until we pulled into the lot and he saw that Tim had already arrived. As dogs will do, he rallied when he saw Tim, so Tim said, "What are we doing here? He looks fine to me". I was unable to explain in so many words how things had gone downhill so quickly that afternoon, so we entered the vet's office deeply divided. Here again, Dr. Revis was a wonder. She let me explain what had happened that day, and then she asked Tim to express his feelings. She understood, and helped him verbalize, that he felt like the rug had been pulled out from under him, and let him vent his anger about the situation. Then she went back over Brinkley's symptoms and offered us the option of keeping him going through the night and Sunday with pain medication and another round of subcutaneous fluids, but added that she felt that if we went that route we would only be back on Monday facing the same decision. That sealed it for both of us and allowed us to get on the same page. We agreed that we could not risk him getting worse overnight, and that we were doing the only humane thing possible for him at that point.

Tim left the room to go out and see if my parents wanted to come in and tell Brinkley goodbye. They all returned together, and Dad went first, then Mom stroked his head and told him how beautiful he was, breaking away in tears. After Mom and Dad left the room, Dr. Revis and Jeanice returned with the medication to put Brinkley into a slumber like what he would have had prior to surgery. We lifted him onto the table and when Dr. Revis administered the shot, our stoic little boy did let out just a little cry; I was so hoping that he wouldn't do that, but I think it also just reaffirmed my knowledge of how tired he was of the entire range of medications and treatments. Then before we knew it, he was sound asleep and we lifted him back down onto the floor. Dr. Revis and Jeanice left the room so Tim and I could be alone with Brinkley to say our final goodbyes in private. Tim went first, rubbing his head, neck and ears and burying his nose in his fur. He told his little boy that he loved him. Then he stood up, and I got down on the floor with my baby. I laid down next to his sleeping body, curling myself around him like I always had at home when we slept on the big doggy bed together. I buried my nose in his beautiful, soft fur, wishing there was some way to keep the scent of it in my nose forever. I told him that he was my boy…that he would always be my boy. Tim encouraged me to go ahead and get up, but I took all the time I needed, snuggling him and kissing him. When I felt ready, I got up, finally letting loose my tears, and let them flow until I could calm myself. We spent a moment gathering our composures, and then Tim went out to get Dr. Revis again.

Dr. Revis had told us that we did not need to stay for the final stage of the procedure, where she would actually put Brinkley to sleep, but we both wanted to be there for him to the end. She and Jeanice came in and we left the room while they placed the IV catheter. Dr. Revis had told us that this might take a while, since Brinkley was a hard stick, and it did seem forever until she opened the door again to let us know we could come back in. We stood with our hands on his sleeping body while Dr. Revis administered the drug that would release him from his suffering forever. Before long she checked his heart and let us know that he had passed. Then she left us alone with him again, and we said goodbye once more. As we left the room for the last time, I looked back, and then wished that I had not, because the final image lingers still in my mind, and this time I knew that he was not just asleep, but had now actually departed from us.

Dr. Revis came out and hugged us, in tears herself, but reassuring us that we had done the right thing for him. We joined my parents in the parking lot, and as we left the vet's office, I noticed the perfect, beautiful crescent moon in the night sky. I pointed it out to my Mom, feeling the assurance as I always do when God sends a lovely sign to let us know that our loved one is now in a much better place. Sadness is only for those of us who are left behind to miss them; they are well, healthy and whole again. We returned home to the quiet of our house, now without Brinkley. We took down and put away some of his things immediately, but other things we left. Unable to wind down, we stayed up until 2:00 AM, finally turning in out of exhaustion, but as it had been when we lost Murphy, peace and rest remained elusive. That first night I found it impossible to release that last mental image of him, and I wondered how I would ever get past it.

Sunday morning dawned bright and sunny, with no indication of the grief that we had just suffered. God was even gracious enough to send me another sign that Brinkley was now at Rainbow Bridge, where all of our pets await us until we join them in Heaven; as I went out the back door to see where Tim was, an extraordinarily bright and beautiful yellow finch came flying up towards me on our deck, practically hovered in mid-air as he neared the balcony pillar, then landed on the outdoor fountain that Brinkley had loved to drink from and got a drink himself. Later, Tim and I decided to spend some time on our porch, even though it was now a much different place without our little guy, then dressed and went out for breakfast, thinking that might provide a distraction. As we left Cracker Barrel, we ran into my friend Trudy while paying our bill; she was picking up a carryout order. And so I got to tell her in person what had happened, and she hugged us both and told us how sorry she was; Trudy and my other friends from Hobbico had all been Brinkley's aunts, and they loved him deeply too. This again was a sign of God's providence, that I would run into her at such a time as this, and that I could share my grief with my close friend and sister in Christ.

I knew that nothing would ever be the same without Brinkley, but I did feel that he had granted me the complete assurance that I had done all I could for him, including that final decision to let him go and release him from his suffering. And on Sunday evening, I also discovered a way to let go of that final image of him from the vet's office. Whenever it entered my mind, I immediately replaced it with the image of him running across Rainbow Bridge, Murphy and Taffy there to greet him, finally free from the pain he had known in his last few weeks on this Earth. I can't bring him back, but I know that one day he will come running to greet me once more, in a place where we will never be parted again.

Epilogue – The Circle of Life

God's perfect timing again…this time, only two days after losing our baby, Tim felt as though Brinkley was leading him to look on the computer for a new little buddy to love. He had done a little half-hearted searching for cocker spaniels in towns nearby, but none seemed promising. Then, on Monday night upon arriving home from work, he got on the computer and just typed in "cocker spaniel breeders", which brought up a web site called cocker-spaniels.com, or C&J Cocker Spaniels. When the site came up, a version of "Happy Days Are Here Again" began to play, along with an invitation to view the parade of cocker spaniel puppies currently available for adoption. Tim was scrolling through the photos when I arrived home from work. We were both surprised at the number of pups available from different litters and all with different dates that they would be ready to go home. We decided to place a call to the gentleman with the web site to ask some general questions about the puppies, and when Joe picked up the phone, he had a wonderful, friendly manner about him, and you could feel his genuine affection for the breed. We asked him about the health and longevity of his dogs and were told that they were free of the genetic issues that our other dogs had dealt with, and that their expected life span was fourteen to seventeen years. That sounded great to us, since Taffy had lived that long, but Murphy and Brinkley only twelve years. Joe seemed to have a more old-time, common sense approach to raising dogs, which we found refreshing and hopeful. We told him we would have another look at the pups on the web site and call him back if we saw one we liked. When we hung up with Joe, I called my Mom and Dad, full of excitement about the puppies, and Mom said they would be right over. By that time, Tim and I had already selected a litter fathered by a dog named McGee, with a mother by the name of Curley Q...too cute! We were on the fence about which puppy to choose...I liked one by the name of NcNew and Tim favored his brother McMack. Their litter mates included McLee, McDee, McMee and McDoodle...all boys! When Mom and Dad arrived, they liked the web site too, and the opinions expressed by Joe. As we sat around the kitchen table listening to "Happy Days Are Here Again", Mom agreed with me that she liked McNew best, so we called Joe back and put him on speaker phone. When we told him which puppy we had chosen, he said, in his big, booming voice, "Wonderful NcNew"! He seemed as pleased with our selection as we were sure we would be! And so the adoption was completed on that phone call, and plans were made to pick up our puppy in a couple weeks when we began our vacations. Joe lives in Miller, Missouri, near Springfield, so we would have about a six hour trip each way, but since we had planned a stay-cation anyway this year, a little road trip with no overnight stay sounded like fun, especially with a puppy awaiting our arrival and coming home to live with us in his new forever home. We planned to go pick him up on

Saturday, July 27th, but then I had an idea. Tim was to begin his vacation on Wednesday, July 24th, so I decided to ask Laura and Hollie if I could get a couple extra days and start my time off on Thursday, July 25th. That way we could go get our boy a couple days early and have more time at home to get him acclimated. Lucky for me, Laura and Hollie are dog lovers, too, and were agreeable to the idea! So I called Joe back to see if we could come early, and he was fine with it too since the puppies were born on May 17th and ready to go home on July 12th. God's timing, again, was unbelievable… that a litter of little red cocker spaniel pups would be born and ready to go home just one day before we lost the love of our lives. It did seem, indeed, like Brinkley wanted us to go on and be happy again, just as Murphy had. And that God, whose mercies are new every morning, was going to provide us with a new little friend to help heal our broken hearts. I was especially concerned about my Mom, who has never gotten over any of our wonderful dogs, and seems to feel the pain afresh whenever she thinks of them. We were hoping that this new little guy would give us a fresh sense of hope.

Thursday, July 25th rolled around at last, and Tim and I got up at 5:00 AM in order to leave town by 6:00 and arrive at our destination around noon. The week ahead looked picture perfect for getting our puppy used to his new home; cooler than normal for July and sunny most days on the projected forecast. The trip went well and we arrived according to schedule, and Joe greeted us from the puppy delivery building next to his house and kennels. We had a pleasant and informative visit while getting acquainted with our new puppy, whom we had decided to name Moxie, which means "common sense". This was the approach we intended to take in raising him, so we chose that name for that reason in combination with its cuteness! And just like our six week visit with Brinkley when we first observed the mass of curls that had developed in his golden brown coat, Moxie gave us quite a surprise upon our first meeting; when Joe handed him to me, I exclaimed, "Oh, look! Half of his left eye is blue!" We had never seen this in a cocker spaniel before and were just delighted with this special feature! We spent about an hour with Joe, took a few pictures, and then got back on the road home, again right on schedule, about 2:00 PM. Moxie was so good on the way home, just fussing a little bit upon leaving the only home he had known up to this moment, then settling in on my lap with his perfectly rounded little head resting in between our two McDonald's cups in my car console! He slept that way for the majority of the ride home, and it just amazed us how well he handled that very long car ride. As we neared home and the sun began to go down, we received what we felt was another affirmation from God that He would have His Hands upon us and the newest little member of our family…a "sun dog" appeared in the sky just to the right of the sun, a bright, beautiful burst of a rainbow with a little snippet of cirrus cloud right next to it, making it look like a little rocket ship just blasting off. Holding Moxie in my lap, I told him about the significance of the rainbow in the Bible, and how it represents God's covenant with Noah and all of humanity. As I talked softly to Moxie, the sun dog lingered long in the sky, right above our driving route. We took it as a sign of God's blessing and thanked Him from the depths of our hearts for His goodness to us.

As I write this final chapter, Moxie has become the newest member of our family, and has proven to be just the joy we anticipated he would be. After all, if Brinkley sent him to us, how could it be otherwise? Joy begets joy, and no creature on earth does that better than our dogs. As Moxie lies here sleeping on my feet, I thank God for our dogs and for the indescribable blessing each one has been to me. I will never know what I have done to deserve such love, but my dogs, and God Almighty, have bestowed it upon me unconditionally. And I stand in awe of such grace; grace which passes all understanding, and yet may be grasped by simply gazing into the eyes, and therefore the soul, of one of these most beautiful of God's creations.

About the Book

"Little Bits of Joy…& wisdom from a very good dog" is a book for anyone who has ever loved a dog with all their heart, and especially for those who have had the privilege of being the beloved companion to a dog who has the ability to teach them to truly appreciate the innate wonder of life. Brinkley was such a dog. From the moment he joined our family he began to instruct us, beginning with a valuable lesson on starting over and learning to love again after the devastating loss of our previous dog. Over the years he would also lend his wisdom to me as I suffered the loss of the job I was planning to retire from and where all of my closest friends still worked, navigated various health challenges with aging family members, and just generally helped me learn to roll with the changes that had become the new norm for my once very stable life. I have always felt that our dogs model some of God's finest characteristics, such as selflessness and humility, better than many humans, and Brinkley certainly taught me a lot about these traits. And yet, he also had a wonderful sense of humor and the ability to lighten our moods, even in the tough times. Finally, he was even able to teach me how to say goodbye with grace, and to embrace the circle of life as he departed to make his journey to Rainbow Bridge and a new puppy joined us to complete our little family once again. "Little Bits of Joy" is a glimpse into just how rewarding life can be when it is shared with a cherished companion, one who ultimately helps us realize our best selves through our selfless love for others.

Printed in the United States
By Bookmasters